A MAN'S BLESSING

BOOKS BY LEONARDO SCIASCIA

A MAN'S BLESSING

THE COUNCIL OF EGYPT

MAFIA VENDETTA

A MAN'S BLESSING

BY LEONARDO SCIASCIA

TRANSLATED FROM THE ITALIAN BY ADRIENNE FOULKE

HARPER & ROW, PUBLISHERS

NEW YORK AND EVANSTON

FIRST EDITION

LIBRARY OF CONGRESS CATALOG CARD NUMBER: 68-15978

B-S

A MAN'S BLESSING

1   The letter arrived in the afternoon delivery. As usual, the postman laid the particolored sheaf of advertising circulars on the counter first; then, carefully, almost as if there were some danger of its exploding, the letter. It was a yellow envelope; a small white rectangle bearing the printed address had been pasted on it.

"I don't like this letter," the postman said.

The pharmacist glanced up from his paper; he took off his glasses. Bored but also curious, he said, "What?"

"I say, I don't like this letter." With his index finger, he pushed it slowly across the marble counter toward the pharmacist.

Without touching the envelope, the pharmacist leaned

1

over to look at it. Then he stood up, replaced his glasses, and studied it.

"Why don't you like it?"

"It was mailed here in town, last night or early this morning, and the address has been cut out from a sheet of pharmacy stationery."

"That's so," the pharmacist corroborated. He stared at the postman, uneasy and embarrassed, as if he were waiting for some explanation or decision.

"It's an anonymous letter," the postman said.

"An anonymous letter," the pharmacist echoed. He had not touched it yet but this letter, he already sensed, would shatter his domestic life; it was a bolt of lightning flashing down to incinerate a woman, the unbeautiful, slightly faded, slightly slovenly woman who at that moment was in the kitchen preparing to put a roast of kid into the oven for supper.

"They're still a vice with people around here, these anonymous letters," the postman said. He had dropped his mailbag on a chair and propped himself against the counter; he was waiting for the pharmacist to make up his mind to open the letter. He had delivered it intact, had forborne opening it first (taking all necessary precautions, naturally), trusting in the affability and ingenuousness of the recipient. If he opens it and it's got to do with sleeping around, he won't tell me anything, the postman thought. But if it's a threat or something, he'll show it to me. Either way, he was not going to leave without finding out. Time he had and plenty.

"An anonymous letter for me?" the pharmacist said, after a long silence. His voice was surprised and indignant, but his face was terrified: pale, eyes flickering, tiny beads of sweat on his upper lip. Apart from the quivering curiosity that gripped him, the postman shared that amazement and indignation. This was a good man, a feeling, generous man. A man who in his pharmacy gave credit to everyone, and who on the property that had come to him as his wife's dowry let his farmers do as they pleased. As to the wife, the postman had never heard the slightest reflection cast on her.

Abruptly, the pharmacist decided. He picked up the envelope, opened it, unfolded the letter. The postman saw what he had expected to see: the letter was pieced together out of newsprint.

The pharmacist drank his bitter cup in one draught. Two lines. Then, "Well, well," he said. Relieved, almost amused. No sex business, the postman thought, and aloud he said, "What is it? A threat?"

"A threat," the pharmacist confirmed. He handed over the letter. The postman took it greedily and read aloud: "'This letter is your death sentence. To avenge what you have done, you will die.'" He folded the sheet and placed it on the counter. "It's a joke," he said, and he believed what he said.

"It may be a joke, you think?" the pharmacist asked, with a twinge of anxiety.

"What else can it be? A joke. Some people's horns itch them so that they go around playing tricks like this. It isn't the first time. They even do it by telephone."

"That's so," the pharmacist said. "That's happened to me. The phone rings in the middle of the night. I go to answer, and a woman's voice asks whether I've lost a dog. She's found a dog that's half blue and half pink, and somebody's told her it was mine. That's a joke. But this is a death threat."

"Same thing," the postman said, with authority. He picked up his bag and started out. "Don't give it a second thought," he said, by way of farewell.

"I won't," the pharmacist said, but the postman had already gone. He did think about it, however. Pretty heavy-handed for a joke . . . if it was a joke. . . . Yet what else could it be? He had never quarreled with anyone. He did not mix in politics, did not even discuss politics, and how he voted was known to no one but himself: Socialist in national elections, out of family tradition and memories of his youth; Christian Democrat in local elections, out of local patriotism, for when the Christian Democrats were in office they managed to wangle some community benefits from the Government, and also as a safeguard against the income tax threatened by the Leftist parties. But never any political talk. Men on the Right took him for a man of the Right, and those on the Left for a man of the Left. To get involved in politics was a waste of time, in any case; if you didn't know that much, either you found politicking profitable or you'd been born blind. In a word, he lived a quiet life. And this was perhaps the one reason that might have sparked the anonymous letter; such a settled man would make another man who lived in idleness and mischief itch to upset, to frighten him. Or perhaps he should look for a different reason in the one passion he did have, and that was hunting. Everyone knows hunters are a jealous lot. All you need is to have a good ferret or a good dog, and every other hunter in town hates you, even men who are your friends, who go hunting with you, who come every evening to sit around the pharmacy and talk. Hunting dogs poisoned—how many cases of that there'd been in town. Owners—owners of the finest dogs, that is—who dared let them run free in the square of an evening risked finding them curled up dead. Strychnine. And someone, who knows, might put two and two together and link strychnine with the pharmacy. Unfairly, of course, unfairly because for Dr. Manno a dog was as sacred as any god, especially the champion hunters, whether his own or his friends'. His own were kept safely out of poison's way. He had eleven hounds, most of them a Cyrenaic breed; cared for like Christians, they were well fed and had the house garden at their disposal for all their needs and for play. They were a pleasure to see, and to hear, too. Their baying made the neighbors grumble sometimes, but to the ears of the pharmacist it was music. He could distinguish each dog's voice and determine the condition of each, whether he was happy or off his feed or suffering from a touch of distemper.

Oh, no, what other explanation could there be? It was a joke, but a joke up to a point. Someone wanted to frighten him, so that on Wednesday, which was his free day, he would not go hunting. All modesty aside, what with his dogs' prowess and his own infallible aim, every Wednesday was a massacre of hares and rabbits. To this Dr. Roscio, his customary companion, could testify. Roscio was also a good marksman, also had good dogs, but even so . . . And thus it was that, in the end, the anonymous letter flattered his vanity: it attested to his fame as a hunter. The season was about to open, as a matter of fact; someone wanted to make him miss out on that first great day which, whether it fell on a Wednesday or not, was for the pharmacist the most glorious day of the year.

Musing on the by now certain intent of the letter and on the identity of its author, the pharmacist pulled out his little wicker chair and sat down in the sliver of shade cast by the houses opposite. Facing him was the bronze statue of Mercuzio Spanò, "DOCTOR OF LAW/UNDERSECRETARY OF THE POSTAL SERVICE." In the harsh afternoon light and in his dual capacity as man of law and custodian of the post, Spanò's shadow stretched out meditatively over all anonymous letters. This mildly ironic fancy occurred to the pharmacist as he glanced up, but then ironic fancy turned quickly into the bitter reflections of a man who, unfairly attacked, discovers how high his own humanity soars above the spitefulness of other men, and who can only reproach and commiserate with himself that he should be so incapable of malice.

As the shadow of Mercuzio Spanò touched the walls of the Castello dei Chiaromonte, which stood on the opposite side of the little square, the pharmacist was so lost in his own thoughts that Don Luigi Corvaia believed him asleep. "Wake up!" he shouted, and the pharmacist started, smiled, and rose to fetch a chair for Don Luigi.

"What a day!" Don Luigi sighed, collapsing into the chair.

"The thermometer hit ninety," the pharmacist said.

"But the air's getting fresher now. You'll see, tonight we'll need a blanket."

"Who can make head or tail of anything any more, even the weather," the pharmacist said bitterly. And he decided to tell his news immediately, so that Don Luigi could take care of passing it along to all the friends who would stop by. "I've received an anonymous letter," he said.

"An anonymous letter?"

"A threat." He rose to go get it.

The reaction of Don Luigi upon reading those two tremendous lines was first "Christ!" and then "It's a joke." The pharmacist agreed that it was a joke; a joke, yes, but perhaps with a purpose.

"What purpose?"

"To keep me from hunting."

"Eh, yes, that's possible. You hunters are capable of anything." Don Luigi decried hunting as being unreasonably expensive and strenuous, while fully appreciating stewed pheasant and sweet-and-sour rabbit.

"Not all hunters," the pharmacist corrected him.

"Of course, of course. Every rule has its exceptions. But you know what some of you are capable of. Strychnine in the meatball, the shot aimed at the friend's dog instead of at the rabbit the dog is chasing. . . . You're indecent. What's the dog done to you, I'd like to know. Good or bad, a dog's a dog. If you people had the stuff it takes, you should have it out with the master."

"It's not the same thing." On occasion, the pharmacist

had known flashes of envy with regard to the dogs of others
—but never, of course, to the extent of wishing them dead.

"To me it's the same thing. A man who's capable of
killing a dog in cold blood will be capable of killing a
Christian as easily as he'd recite the Lord's Prayer. But," he
added, "perhaps that's because I'm no hunter."

They discussed the psychology of hunters virtually the
whole evening, because each new arrival was told the whole
story anew, beginning with the anonymous letter and con-
cluding with the dark jealousy, envy, and worse, of all those
who practiced the ancient and honorable sport of hunting.
Excepting those present, naturally, although Don Luigi Corvaia entertained suspicions even of those present, both as
regarded the poisoning of dogs and the anonymous letter.
From under wrinkled lids, his sharp little eyes scrutinized
their faces. Dr. Roscio; Pecorilla, the notary; Rosello, the
lawyer; Professor Laurana; the pharmacist himself (who
could be not only a dog-poisoner but also the author of the
letter, thereby supplying himself with a testimonial to his
being a fearsome hunter). In a word, Don Luigi, bred in the
ways of mistrust, suspicion, and malice, was prepared to at-
tribute to each man as much spitefulness as his own mind
secretly distilled.

All were agreed, however, in adjudging that the letter
should be taken as a joke; malevolent in any circumstances,
and worse still if it really aimed at keeping the pharmacist
away from the formal opening day of the hunting season.
When the marshal of the carabinieri passed by, as he did
every evening, the pharmacist was quite prepared to turn the
whole thing into a joke. Facetiously pretending that he was

in the grip of fear and prostration, he lamented the fact that in a town protected by the marshal an honest person, a good citizen, a decent family man, should be threatened with death just like that.

"What's happened?" the marshal asked. Expecting some absurd revelation, he looked amused already. But he became serious when he was shown the letter. It could be a joke; perhaps no doubt it was a joke, but the offense existed, and it had to be reported.

"What do you mean, reported!" said the pharmacist, who was by now euphoric.

"Oh, yes, there must be a report. That's the law. All right, I'll save you the trouble of coming over to the barracks, and we'll write it out here. But it must be done. It takes only a minute."

They went inside. The pharmacist lighted the lamp that stood on the counter and began to write as the marshal dictated.

As the marshal was dictating, he was holding the letter open, so that the light of the lamp fell slantingly on it. Professor Laurana, who was curious about the form and language of the complaint, clearly saw the word "*Unicuique*" emerge through the reverse side of the paper and then, in smaller letters, confusedly, "natural order . . . *menti observantur* . . . time . . . seat." He moved closer the better to decipher the words, and read aloud "human," whereupon the marshal was annoyed and, defending what was from now on a secret of his office, said, "Please, don't you see that I am dictating?"

"I was reading the back of the clipping," the professor

said to excuse himself. The marshal dropped his hand and folded the letter.

"It might be a good idea if you were to examine it that way, too." The professor was a bit miffed.

"We will do all that is necessary, you may be sure," the marshal said haughtily. And he resumed his dictation.

2   August 23, 1964, was the last blessed day pharmacist Manno spent on this earth. According to the coroner, he lived it through to sunset. In support of the medical evidence, there was, furthermore, the game that spilled from his and Dr. Roscio's bags: eleven rabbits, six partridges, three hares. According to those qualified to judge, that was a full day's kill, considering the fact that the area was not a game preserve and not really rich in wildlife. The pharmacist and the doctor liked their hunting to be a challenge, to test their own and their dogs' strength; that is why they got along well and always went out together, without looking for other companions. And they ended that happy hunting day together, only thirty

11

feet apart—the pharmacist shot between the shoulders, the doctor in the chest. Also, one of the dogs stayed to keep them company, whether in the everlasting void or the celestial hunting grounds. It was one of the ten the pharmacist had taken with him, having left the eleventh at home because of an eye inflammation. Perhaps the dog had rushed upon the assassins, or perhaps they had killed him out of a surplus of passion and ferocity.

The pharmacist's nine other dogs and the doctor's two got away; for the moment, no one knew how. But the fact of the matter was that around nine o'clock they came back to town running in close ranks, according to town legend, and howling so weirdly that everyone (because everyone, naturally, saw and heard them) shivered with a fearful presentiment. Trooped together thus and whimpering, the dogs headed like a shot for the storehouse that the pharmacist had converted into a kennel; there, before the closed door, they redoubled their howls, no doubt communicating to their comrade who had remained behind with his eye inflammation news of the tragic happening.

This return of the dogs set the whole town to disputing for days and days (as will always happen when people discuss the nature of dogs) about the order of Creation, since it is not at all fair that dogs should lack the gift of speech. No account was taken, in the Creator's defense, that even had they had the gift of speech, the dogs would, in the given circumstances, have become so many mutes both with regard to the identity of the murderers and in testifying before the marshal of the carabinieri. When the marshal was informed of the disturbing return of the dogs, around

midnight, he was already in bed. Until dawn, aided by his
police and various idlers, he stood in the square trying to
persuade the animals, with tidbits of tripe, exhortations, and
haranguings, to lead him to the spot where they had left
their masters. But the dogs cared not a whit. Accordingly,
the sun was already high when, having learned from the wife
of the pharmacist the name of the region where the two
men had presumably gone to hunt, the marshal set out in
search of them; and only at vespers—may God spare him
another such day—did he return with the bodies. In the
condition he had expected, for the moment he leaped from
his bed, he had foreseen the realization of the threat con-
tained in the letter that everyone, himself included, had
taken for a joke.

It was a big headache, the biggest that had ever beset the
marshal in the three years he had spent in that town: a
double homicide, the victims two decent, respected, well-
liked persons, both in prominent positions; men with prominent relatives, the pharmacist on his wife's side (she being
a Spanò, the grandniece of the Spanò memorialized in
bronze), and Dr. Roscio, on his side the son of Professor
Roscio, the famous eye specialist, and on his wife's side, she
born a Rosello, niece of the dean and a cousin of the lawyer
Rosello.

Needless to say, the colonel and chief inspector of the
squadra mobile hurried down from the county seat. And
then, as everyone read in his paper, the inspector took over
direction of the investigation, with, of course, the complete
cooperation of the carabinieri. The first step—since rain
always falls on wet ground—was to round up everyone with

a prison record, excluding swindlers and loan sharks, of which there were quite a few in town. But in the space of forty-eight hours all those who had been detained were restored to their families. There was an absolute dearth of clues; even the carabinieri's stool pigeons were completely in the dark. Meanwhile, preparations for the funerals were under way, and on a grandiose scale, as befitted the position of the victims and their families, the widespread interest in the case, and the sympathy of the citizenry. Additionally, the police decided to solemnize and eternalize the ceremonies by filming them, and their preparations to that end were made in such secrecy that not one of those who walked in the funeral procession failed to appear in the film with a face that seemed to be saying to the camera's eye, to the cameraman, and to all investigators, "I know you're there, but you're wasting your time. Mine is the face of a gentleman, an innocent man, and a friend of the victims."

As they followed the dead, who were borne on the shoulders of their more devoted and robust clients and who weighed like lead because the caskets of massive walnut were, in the bargain, incrusted with bronze, the friends of the pharmacy circle discussed the letter and ransacked the pharmacist's past, bestowing all the sympathy that circumstances called for on poor Dr. Roscio, who had no part in any of it and who had paid with his life for the imprudence of going with the pharmacist on the heels of that threatening letter. Because—with all respect to the pharmacist—confronted now with the atrocious execution of the threat, one had to admit that there must have been some reason that armed the hand of the assassin; an absurd reason, even,

based perhaps on some small, long-past, unintentional deed
(or misdeed) of the victim. And the letter had put it plainly:
for what you have done you will die. So somehow, oh, a
mere nothing, naturally, and naturally long ago, the pharmacist must have been at fault in something. But, on the
other hand, no one does anything for no reason; much less
does one kill a man (two men, in this case, with innocent
Dr. Roscio caught in the middle) for a trifle. In a heated
moment, then yes; then one can even kill a man over a
mere nothing, over a word. But this crime was prepared in
cold blood, to avenge an offense that could not easily be
forgotten, one of those offenses that time does not erase but
aggravates. Madmen exist, they abound, agreed; men who
think constantly of some person, who imagine that person
is secretly, constantly bent on persecuting them. But really
can one call this crime the crime of a madman? Quite aside
from the fact that there would have had to be two madmen,
and to think of two madmen acting in accord is rather difficult. And there were two murderers; there had to be two. No
one would have risked confronting alone two armed men,
men who had their guns in hand, loaded and at the ready.
And furthermore both were known to be quite fast, quite
accurate marksmen. Something about the whole thing was
crazy, yes—the letter itself. Why the warning? Suppose the
pharmacist had some wrong on his conscience (and really
he must have had) or suppose he was simply intimidated
by the threat, and in either case suppose he had decided
not to go hunting. That would have spiked the murderers'
plans, would it not?

"The letter," the notary Pecorilla said, "is typical of a

crime of passion. No matter at what risk, the avenger wants his victim to start to die—and at the same time to start to relive his guilt—from the moment he receives the warning."

"But the pharmacist didn't start to die in the slightest," Professor Laurana said. "He was a little upset that evening, maybe, when he got the letter. But later he joked about it, he was perfectly calm."

"And how do you know what feelings a man can hide?"

"Why hide anything? On the contrary, if he had some suspicion about the source of the threat, the most sensible thing to have done—"

"—would have been to inform his friends and even the marshal," the notary ironically completed his sentence for him.

"And why not?"

"But, my dear friend!" the notary said, with amazement and reproach but with affection. "Imagine, my friend, that Dr. Manno of blessed memory, in a moment of weakness, of madness . . . After all, we are human, we are men, no?" He looked around for approval, and no one said him nay. "A pharmacy is frequented more by women than by men, and a pharmacist is considered almost like a physician. What I mean is, opportunity makes the thief. A girl, a young woman . . . But let us be careful, now. It doesn't strike me that the departed had any such weakness. Still— who could take an oath on that?"

"No one," Don Luigi Corvaia said.

"There, you see?" the notary continued. "And I could say also that it so happens—well, that there is something on which a suspicion might . . . Let us be quite clear: the deceased did make a marriage of convenience. All one need do is look at the lady, poor thing, to have no doubts about that. A very good woman, I agree, a woman of many qualities, but ugly, poor creature, as only God could have—"

"He came from a poor family," Don Luigi said, "and like everyone who has been poor, he was greedy and stingy, especially when he was young. Then, after the marriage, with the pharmacy going well, he changed. Outwardly."

"Just so. Outwardly. However, deep inside he was a closed man, a hard man. . . . But to come back to the point, think about this for a moment: How did he behave when there was any talk about women?"

The notary's question received a prompt reply from Don Luigi. "He kept still. He listened, he didn't say a word."

"This—let's frankly admit it—with men like us, who talk about women to a fault, this is the attitude of someone who does not talk but who acts. Sometimes—remember?—he would smile a little, as if to say 'You talk, but I act.' And you must take into account, too, that he was a fine-looking man."

"What you are saying, my dear notary, proves nothing," the professor said. "Even conceding that the pharmacist had seduced a girl or taken advantage of a married woman, to speak like the old-fashioned romances—even if this were true, one would still have to explain why, when he got the letter, he couldn't have confided his suspicions about the identity of the writer to the marshal."

"Because there are times when a man who has to choose between losing peace at home and gaining peace in the

hereafter chooses peace in the hereafter, and that's that,"
Commendatore Zerillo intervened, with a face that bespoke
his regret at having been incapable, to that moment, of making the same choice.

"But the marshal could discreetly—" Professor Laurana
began to object.

"Don't talk nonsense," the notary interrupted. "And
then— Excuse me, I'll explain later. . . ." for they had
reached the place where, before the cemetery church,
speeches in praise of the departed would be delivered, and
the notary had been designated to eulogize the pharmacist.

But the professor did not need the notary's explanations.
He had, he knew, been talking nonsense.

Already the evening before, the widow Manno had, with
exquisite allusions, with delicate euphemisms, been invited
by the police inspector to recall, to reflect whether by any
chance, if ever, as it always and everywhere does happen,
she had had the shadow, the *shadow* of a suspicion not that
her husband had entertained extramarital relations, Heaven
forbid, or that he might have been occasionally unfaithful
to her, but whether some woman might have hovered
around him, tempted him, come too frequently to the pharmacy; the vaguest impression, so to speak, and the inspector
would be satisfied. The woman said no, repeatedly, firmly.
But the inspector did not concede defeat. He had the maid
brought to the police barracks and, by questioning her pa-
ternally, after six hours he managed to get her to admit that,
yes, once there had been a little incident in the family, in
connection with a girl who, to her mistress's way of thinking, was seen too often in the pharmacy. (The pharmacy

was on the first floor, under the family living quarters, and it was easy for the Signora, when she so wished, to observe who came and went.) Question: "And the pharmacist?" Answer: "He denied it." Question: "And you, what did you think?" Answer: "Me? What business was it of mine?" Question: "Did you have the same suspicions as the Signora?" Answer: "The Signora was not suspicious. It seemed to her that the girl was very lively, and a man is a man." Question: "Very lively. And very lovely also, was she not?" Answer: "Not so very, I don't think. But lively, yes." Question: "Very lively. That is, very vivacious, rather flirtatious . . . Is that what you mean to say?" Answer: "Yes." Question: "And what was this girl's name?" Answer: "I don't know." There followed such variants as "I don't know her," "I never saw her," "I saw her once but I don't even remember what she looked like," and so on and on, from two-thirty in the afternoon until seven-fifteen, when, with a sudden greening of memory, the maid recalled not only the name but the age, the street, the house number, the names of relatives extending to cousins thrice removed, and an infinity of other information regarding the girl in question.

Thanks to which, at seven-thirty the girl was before the inspector and her father was waiting outside the entrance to the barracks; and at nine o'clock the future mother-in-law, betaking herself to the girl's home in the company of two women friends, returned one wrist watch, one key chain, one necktie, and twelve letters, and demanded the immediate restitution of one ring, one bracelet, one chapel veil, and twelve letters. This ceremony rapidly disposed of, which dissolved the engagement without remission, the elderly exfuture mother-in-law placed a final, malevolent seal upon its rupture with the exhortation "Find yourselves some other fool," proclaiming by implication that her own son was not intelligent, since he had risked entrusting his honor to someone who had had an intrigue with the pharmacist. The exhortation elicited groans of shame and rage from the girl's mother and relatives, who had come on the run. The old woman, followed by her two friends, left before they could recover and set upon her; the moment she set foot in the street, she shouted, so that the neighborhood might hear, "One man's trouble is another man's blessing. Why couldn't they have killed him before ever my son set foot in that house?"—evidently alluding to the pharmacist, who thus received his second funeral eulogy of the day.

3   On the basis of a stack of prescriptions and the testimony of the doctor who had written them, the inspector was persuaded that the girl's going back and forth to the pharmacy had almost definitely to be attributed to the meningitis that had struck down her brother, a boy of eleven, who still bore the signs of his illness: an imbecilic, terrified air, lapses of memory, and impairment of speech. Since the father went out into the country to work and the mother never left the house, the duty of going to have prescriptions filled and to ask clarifications of the doctor in charge had fallen to her, who was, furthermore, the brightest and best-educated member of the family. Naturally, the father and the ex-fiancé were

21

also questioned, but perfunctorily and by way of closing that channel of the investigation.

The inspector convinced, it remained for the girl to convince an entire town—seven thousand five hundred inhabitants, the members of her family included. They, once she was released by the inspector, descended upon her and, with such good and sufficient cause, silently, steadily, diligently beat her.

Signora Spanò, now the widow Manno, who had fetched out all the photographs of the pharmacist to select the one she would have reproduced in enamel and set in his tombstone, saw in each her husband's handsome, tranquil face animated by a barely perceptible sneer around the lips and the eyes lighted by a cold, derisive gleam. Thus the metamorphosis of the pharmacist was proceeding even under the roof where he had lived for fifteen years as a faithful husband and exemplary father. Tortured by suspicion even in sleep, with a flashing of mirrors in which the pharmacist appeared naked as a worm and disarticulated like a mannequin, the Signora would start awake and, rising from bed, resume her interrogation of her husband's images; and sometimes it seemed that he answered her from the grave where he lay dead, and that everything was dead, that nothing mattered; at other times, and more often, it seemed as if he spoke from the cruel and cynical everyday life that must go on. As for her relatives, they were resolutely disdainful, having always been quick to reproach her for a marriage that they had opposed at the time with every means at their command, while the relatives of the pharmacist—now as far removed from the sumptuous mourning as they had kept themselves from the comfortable, contented life of their relative—they were inclined to consider the recent events in terms of fate; that is, if you change your station in life, if you presume to attain wealth and happiness, then suffering and disgrace and death overtake you all the more quickly.

In the absence of any clue whatever except for a cigar stub found on the scene of the crime (the investigators assumed that during their long wait in ambush one of the assassins had smoked it), there was not one person in town who had not already, privately and to his own satisfaction, solved or almost solved the mystery, or who did not consider that he was in possession of a key to solve it. Professor Laurana had his key; it was the *Unicuique* that, together with other words he had since forgotten, had fortuitously shone through the back of the letter as the slanting light fell on it. He did not know whether the marshal had attached any importance to the suggestion that he study the reverse of the letter or whether now, in the course of the inquiry, in the police laboratories they had examined the letter on both sides, in which case the *Unicuique* could not be other than the focus of the investigations. At heart, he was anything but sure either that they had ever undertaken to examine the letter in the way he had suggested or that, once it was examined, they would recognize the importance of the clue. A certain vanity was in play here, almost as if it were not granted to others to penetrate into such an evident secret or such secret evidence, which, because of the contradiction it implied, required a free and quick mind.

And it was out of vanity that, almost without wishing to, he found himself taking the first step. Passing by the newsstand, as he did every evening, he asked for the "*Osservatore Romano*, please." The news vendor was astonished, partly because the professor enjoyed the reputation, not entirely deserved, of being furiously anticlerical and partly because for at least twenty years no one had ever asked him for the Vatican paper. He said as much, causing the professor's heart to skip a beat for joy. "It's a good twenty years I've not heard anyone asking for the *Osservatore*. During the war, a couple of people read it; five copies used to come in. Then the secretary of the local Fascist Party headquarters came and told me that if I didn't cancel the order for the *Osservatore*, they'd take away my vendor's license. The man who holds the whip makes the rules. What would you have done?"

"What you did," the professor said. And to himself: so no one has asked the newsman whether he sells the *Osservatore*. But perhaps the marshal already knows. I'll have to try the post office or the postman.

The postmaster was a loquacious fellow, everybody's friend. There was no need to waste time in getting the information. "I'm preparing a paper on Manzoni. Someone's told me about an article that appeared in the *Osservatore Romano* two weeks or so ago. Does anyone here in town subscribe to the *Osservatore*?"

It was common knowledge that the professor wrote little critical essays and had them published in magazines. So the postmaster gave the information without a thought. (He would not have given it, or he would have given it hesitatingly, suspiciously, had the police already asked him about it.) "Two copies come in. One for Dean Rosello and one for the rector of Sant'Anna's."

"What about Christian Democratic headquarters?"

"No."

"Not even for the secretary?"

"Not even for him. Just two copies, you can be sure." And ascribing the professor's insistence to a lack of familiarity with priests, he advised, "Go to the rector of Sant'-Anna's. If he has the issue you're looking for, he'll certainly let you have it."

The professor followed the advice forthwith. The Church of Sant'Anna was two steps away, with the rectory to one side. For that matter, he was on rather friendly terms with the rector, a very freethinking man who was detested by his superiors and cherished by the people. (His superiors were nonetheless right.)

The professor was received with open arms, but when he explained the reason for his visit, the rector looked regretful and said that, yes, he did get the *Osservatore*, that out of inertia—and also to avoid attracting attention—he had never canceled the subscription taken out by his predecessor; but as for reading it, well . . . "I've never read it, not even opened it. I think my chaplain walks off with it. You know him? That young priest who's all bones, never looks you in the eye? He's an idiot. And a spy, too; that's why they saddled me with him. Oh, he reads the *Osservatore*; he may even keep it. If you like, I'll phone him."

"I'd appreciate it."

"Right away." He lifted the receiver and gave the number. The moment someone answered, he asked abruptly, "Have you made the daily report to the Dean?" He winked at the professor, holding the receiver away from his ear, and the other's voice came over the wire, surely saying no. Then, "Oh, I don't give a— Anyhow, that's not why I'm calling you. Now, listen to me. What do you do with all those copies of the *Osservatore Romano* that you steal from me?" More protestations, which the rector cut short, saying, "No, this time I'm joking. Come on, now, tell me what you do with them. . . . You keep them? . . . Good, good. . . . Wait a moment, I'll tell you which dates I need—no, not for me, naturally, for a friend, a professor. . . . Which issues do you need?"

"I don't know exactly. I'd say that the article I'm looking for would have appeared between July 1st and August 15th."

"All right. . . . Listen, have you got the issues from July 1st to August 15th? . . . You have to check? Well, check. And at the same time see whether there's anything there about Manzoni. Check carefully, now, and call me back." He hung up and explained, "He's looking. If he finds the issue, I'll tell him to bring it to me tomorrow morning. That way, you spare yourself the displeasure of having to see him. He's a filthy animal."

"Really?"

"It takes a strong stomach, believe me, to have him anywhere near. He's got his little vices, too, in my opinion. You know what I mean. . . . I get a kick out of keeping him surrounded by girls. How he suffers, the poor devil, how he suffers! And he takes his revenge. As you know, I take life foursquare. . . . Did you ever hear the story about the priest who had a housekeeper who was a virgin and whose bishop investigated him? . . . No? I want to tell it to you. For once you'll hear a priest tell a story about priests. . . . So people come to tell the bishop that in some town or other there is this priest who not only keeps a housekeeper much younger than the regulations allow—*lupus in fabula*, as Manzoni says about the synodalist—but who tucks her into bed beside him. Naturally, the bishop comes on the run. He bursts into the priest's house, sees the housekeeper, who really is young and quite pretty, then the bedroom, with a bed as wide as a city block. He accuses the priest. The priest denies nothing. 'It is true, Your Excellency,' he says. 'She sleeps on this side and I sleep on that side. But do you see those hinges there on the wall between her side and mine? Every evening before going to bed, I attach this plank —it's as big and strong as a wall,' and he points to the plank. The bishop softens; such candor amazes him; he is reminded of those saints in the Middle Ages who used to go to bed with a woman but put a cross or sword between them. And he says, very gently, 'But, my son, the plank, yes, no doubt, that's a precaution. But what about temptation, what if temptation, as wild and mad and hellish as it is, assails you? What do you do when temptation assails you?' 'Oh, Excellency,' the priest replies, 'it doesn't take all that much strength to raise the plank.' "

The rector had time to tell one or two more stories before the call came from his chaplain. He had checked; he had all copies of the paper from July 1st to August 15th, but the article on Manzoni wasn't in any of them.

"I'm sorry," the rector said, "but perhaps he didn't know how to look. I told you he's an idiot. To make sure, maybe you should go see for yourself. Or do you want me to tell him to bring all the papers here to me?"

"Oh, no, thank you, that would be too much of a nuisance. It isn't as if the article were indispensable to me."

"I can believe that. It's ages since we've said anything indispensable. And about Manzoni—well, imagine what a Catholic has to say about Manzoni. If you're going to understand, to love Manzoni today, you must be a libertine, a real libertine, in both the original and current sense of the word."

"But there are Catholics who've written illuminating things about Manzoni."

"I know—the God that destroys and restores, grace, landscape, Manzoni and Vergil. . . . Oh, as far as that goes, I would say that the whole of Manzoni criticism has been written by Catholics. With a few exceptions, and none of them very intelligent, to tell the truth. And do you know when you come close to the core of it, to the magma? When you come to the theme of the silence of love. . . . But that's enough of that. . . . Look, I want to show you something, because you understand such things, I know." He went to a wall closet, opened it, and took out a small statue, a San Rocco. "Look at this. What movement, eh? And what delicacy. . . . Do you know how I got it? From a colleague of mine, in a town not far from here. He had it in his sacristy—kept it in a chest where he'd tossed it like a piece of old rubbish. I bought him a beautiful big new San Rocco—of papier-mâché. He thinks I'm a maniac, someone who's crazy about any old junk. It almost hurt his conscience to come out so much better on the swap."

The rector was rather famous for being a sharp and rapacious connoisseur of objets d'art, and he was known to maintain constant—and profitable—dealings with some antiquarian in Palermo. In fact, now showing the San Rocco from every angle: "I've already shown him, and they're offering me three hundred thousand lire. But for the moment I want to enjoy him myself a little. There's time enough for him to end up in the house of some thief who steals from the public purse. . . . What do you think? First half of the sixteenth century, wouldn't you say?"

"I'd say so, yes."

"That's what Professor De Renzis thinks, too. He's an authority on Sicilian sculpture of the fifteenth and sixteenth centuries, you know. Only his opinion"—he burst out laughing—"always coincides with mine, since I pay him."

"You don't believe in anything," the professor said.

"Oh, yes, in some things. In too many things, maybe, considering the times we live in."

Everyone in town knew the story, possibly true, about the time he was celebrating Mass and how, when he came to open the Tabernacle, the key got stuck in the lock. As the rector was wrestling with the key, the imprecation slipped out: "What the devil's wrong here?" The fact is, he was always in a hurry over church business and always had unlimited time for his wheeling and dealing.

"But—excuse me for saying this—I don't understand—" the professor began.

"—why I wear these robes? Let me tell you, I didn't put them on of my own free will. You know the story, by any chance? . . . An uncle of mine was a priest, rector of this church, in fact. A moneylender. Rich. Left me all he had on condition that I become a priest. I was three years old when he died. At ten, when I entered the seminary, I felt like Saint Louis himself, and at twenty-two, when I left, like the Devil incarnate. I'd have liked to throw up the whole business, but there was the inheritance, and there was my mother. Today I don't care about what I inherited and my mother's dead. I could leave—"

"But there's the Concordat."

"In my case, with my uncle's will in hand, the Concordat wouldn't hurt me. I became a priest under coercion, so they'd let me go without taking away any of my civil rights. But the fact is, at this point I'm comfortable in these robes, and as between comfort and guilt I've struck a perfect balance—and a full life."

"But don't you risk running into trouble?"

"No, absolutely not. Let them try to touch me and I'll raise such a scandal for them that the correspondents of *Pravda*, even, will come down and camp here for a month. But what am I saying, a scandal? A whole series, a fireworks display!"

Thus agreeably entertained, Professor Laurana left the

rector around midnight. He went off filled with friendly sentiments for the rector of Sant'Anna. "But," he said to himself, "Sicily and maybe all Italy is full of likable people who should have their heads chopped off."

As for *Unicuique*, he had learned that it could not have been clipped from the paper that went to the parish of Sant'Anna. And that was already something.

4   The three days of deep mourning had passed, and therefore Laurana felt he would be committing no indiscretion in going to Dean Rosello, to ask for the loan of the copy of the *Osservatore Romano* between the first of July and the fifteenth of August that carried an article on Manzoni which he urgently needed in his work. The Dean was the uncle of Dr. Roscio's widow, and devoted to her, for the girl had grown up and lived in his home until the day of her marriage. The deanery was a great house, supported by large and undivided property holdings. Some twenty years before, when two married brothers lived there with their families, twelve people formed a single household, together with the Dean, who was its head not merely in the spiritual sense. Then death and marriages had removed nine people, so that four remained: the Dean, two sisters-in-law, and one nephew, a bachelor still, who was Rosello the lawyer.

The Dean was in the sacristy, removing his robes after Mass. He welcomed the professor warmly, almost as if Heaven had sent him. After ten minutes of polite conversation, they got around to speaking of the fearful crime, the gentle and generous nature of the departed Dr. Roscio, and the inconsolable grief of his widow.

"A terrible crime. And so mysterious, so baffling," the professor said.

"Not so mysterious," the Dean said.

There was a pause. Then: "You see, that man—the poor pharmacist, I mean—had his little affairs. No one knew anything, I agree. The fact remains, he was first warned and then killed, and this is the typical revenge pattern. My poor nephew bore the brunt of it."

"Do you think so?"

"But what else can one think? Conflicts of interest the man had with no one, so far as anyone has been able to discover. One can think, then, only of an intrigue. And of a father or a brother or a fiancé who, at a certain moment, is enflamed by the offense and puts an end to it. With such fury that he does not even notice there is an innocent man caught in the middle."

"That is possible, but it's not certain."

"Certain? But, my dear professor, what is certain except for God? And death. Certain it is not, I agree, but factors that can bring us close to certainty are there. First: the let-

ter warns the pharmacist that he will pay with his life for the
wrong he has done; it does not say what wrong, but whoever
wrote the letter either assumed that the memory of that
wrong, even if it was done long ago, must instantly leap to
the mind of the man who committed it—a grave wrong,
therefore, since it was unforgettable—or he knew that he
was referring to something recent, something current, so to
speak. Second: as you well know, since they have told me
you were present, if the pharmacist did not want to report
the letter to the police, he must at the very least have suspected the report might lead to something that would reflect
little credit on him; he must have at least suspected this.
Third: it does not seem that life in the pharmacist's family
ran too smoothly—"

"I don't know. . . . But I would have some objections
to raise. First: the pharmacist receives a clear, direct threat.
And what does he do? Within a week, he offers his enemy
the best possible opportunity for carrying out the threat: he
goes hunting. The truth is, he didn't take it seriously; he
thought it was a joke. *Ergo*, no guilt, past or present. Or
better, since the threat was carried out so ferociously, one
should think in terms of some harm done a long, long time
ago, so long ago that revenge so long delayed seemed incredible. Or yet again, one would have to think of some wrong
committed inadvertently—a gesture, a word, something to
which the one person pays no attention but which indelibly
wounds a sick, overwrought mind. Second: no one who saw
the letter thought it was to be taken seriously. No one. And
this is a small town where it is very hard for a relationship
no matter how secret, or for a vice no matter how hidden,

to escape notice. As for his not wanting to report the letter, that's true, but that was because he and his friends construed it as a joke."

"You may be right," the Dean said, but one could read in his eyes that he held firmly to his own opinion. Then he prayed, "Dear Lord, cast down Thy light and discover unto us the truth, for the sake of justice, and not of vengeance."

"Let's hope so," the professor said, by way of amen. Then he explained his reason for coming to disturb his host.

"The *Osservatore Romano*," the Dean said with relish, delighted that a nonbeliever should need it. "Yes, I do get it, I read it, but as for keeping it . . . I keep magazines—*Civiltà Cattolica, Vita e Pensiero*—but not the newspapers. The sacristan goes for the mail and brings it to me here; then I take any private letters and the papers home. Once I've read the papers, they pass, how shall I say, under the jurisdiction of the household. The *Osservatore Romano, Il Popolo* . . . here, see"—from a pile of mail he pulled the *Osservatore Romano*—"now I shall take this home and read it directly after lunch, and surely by this evening my sisters-in-law or the maid will use it to wrap something or to light a fire. Unless there is an encyclical or an address or a decree of His Holiness, of course."

"Of course."

"If this copy, which is from the day before yesterday, is of any use to you"—he held it out, still folded—"I can glance through it quickly here. For that matter, I am in arrears even with the papers. This last week has been an inferno for me. . . ."

Laurana had opened the paper and was looking with delight at the masthead. There it was—*Unicuique*—exactly as it had appeared through the reverse side of the letter. *Unicuique suum:* to each his own. A handsome type face, the descender of the "q" elegantly hooked. Then the crossed keys and the triple crown and, in the same type face, *Non Praevalebunt.* To each his own . . . and likewise to the pharmacist and Dr. Roscio. What lay behind that *Unicuique* which the same hand that later snuffed out two lives had clipped and pasted on a sheet of paper? The word "sentence"? The word "death"? What a pity he could not get another look at the letter now lying in a confidential police folder.

"Don't hesitate," the Dean was saying. "If this copy is of any use to you, do take it."

"I beg your pardon? . . . Oh, yes, thank you. But, no, no, it isn't of any help to me." He laid the paper on the table and stood up. Suddenly he was upset, unable to endure the smell the sacristy exuded of old wood, faded flowers, and wax. "I am very grateful to you," he said, holding out his hand, which the Dean pressed between both his own with all the love owed to the strayed lambs. "Until another time, for I do hope you will come to see me occasionally," the Dean said, in parting. "With much pleasure," Laurana replied.

He left the sacristy and walked through the deserted church. The square in front offered not one patch of shade; as he crossed it, he reflected how comfortable life was in church and sacristy, and the reflection shifted into an ironic extension—comfortable for the rector of Sant'Anna as for the Dean. They were comfortable, each in his own way. Or perhaps, going by what people said, both in the same way, only the appearances being different. His mind wandered; out of a kind of subtle, unconscious self-love, he was evading the point that spelled disappointment and defeat. The point was this: even were he to ascertain from which number of the *Osservatore* the *Unicuique* had been clipped and then pasted onto the letter, it would be impossible to trace where that copy of the paper had gone once it left the Dean's house. Because the idea that the Dean, his sisters-in-law, his nephew, or maid could have any part in this—why, that was unthinkable. As to what use was made of the paper after the Dean had perused it, one could envisage a minimum number of readers who, like the chaplain of Sant'Anna, might collect it; but as the wrapping for a package, how could one possibly determine how that particular piece of that particular issue might have reached the author of the letter (and of the crimes)? Not to mention the fact that in the county seat the paper was sold on newsstands and anyone, whether casually or for a specific purpose, could have bought it.

All in all, the police had shown good sense in paying no attention to the *Unicuique*. Experience counts, say what you will. A waste of time to go looking for a needle in a haystack when you know it is a needle without an eye, a needle through which you cannot thread a way into the next stage of the investigation. But he had been dazzled by that detail. A newspaper that had only two subscribers in the whole town: a precise clue that opened up a straight path for the investigation. And it led, instead, to a blind alley.

Not that the police, who had latched on to the cigar stub,

were betting on a better card. The brand had been verified; it was a Branca. The only person who smoked Brancas was the town clerk, a man who was not only above all suspicion but was a stranger and had lived in town for only six months. "The *Osservatore* is worth the Branca," Laurana told himself. "But let the police run after the cigar, and you forget all about the *Osservatore*." At home, however, while his mother was setting the table for lunch, he jotted down in a little notebook: "The person who composed the letter by cutting the words out of the *Osservatore* (a) bought the paper in the county seat for shrewd reasons of his own, intending to add confusion to the search, or (b) that particular paper happened to be at hand, and he did not even realize what paper he was using, or (3) he was so accustomed to seeing that paper around him that he considered it just another paper, and gave no thought to its distinctive typography and to its limited, almost professional distribution." He laid down his pen, reread the note, then tore the paper into tiny shreds.

5 Paolo Laurana, professor of Italian
and history in the classical *liceo* in the
county seat, was considered by his students to be an odd but
good sort, and by the fathers of the students to be a good
but odd sort. The term "odd," in the judgment of both sons
and fathers, was meant to denote a strangeness that did not
achieve the bizarre; it was something opaque, dense, almost
repressed. His strangeness, nonetheless, made his superior
competence weigh more lightly on the boys, and at the
same time forestalled the fathers from finding the handle
that would incline him not to clemency but to justice (since,
need it be said, the boy no longer exists who deserves to be
flunked). He was mild to the point of timidity, to the point

of stammering; when they appealed to him, he seemed to attach great importance to what they said. But by now it was recognized that his gentleness concealed a firm decisiveness, an unmovable judgment; the appeals that went in one ear came out the other.

For the whole school year, his life was divided between town and county seat. He left on the seven-o'clock and returned on the two-o'clock bus. The afternoon he devoted to reading and studying; he spent the early evening at the club or the pharmacy; he returned home around eight. He gave no private lessons; not even in the summer, when he preferred to busy himself with his literary criticism, which was published in magazines that no one in the town read.

An honest, meticulous, melancholy man; not very intelligent, and indeed at times positively obtuse; with frustrations and resentments that he recognized and deplored; not without a certain self-consciousness, a secret vanity and arrogance that came to him both from the school milieu where, because of his training and erudition, he felt—and was—so different from his colleagues, and from the isolation in which he as a man of culture, so to speak, found himself. In politics, he was considered by everyone to be a Communist, but he was not. In his personal life, he was considered to be the victim of his mother's jealous and possessive love, and this was true. Although almost forty, he was still given to indulging in secret crushes on students and teachers who were not at all, or hardly, aware of it. The girl or colleague had only to show some response to his infatuation for him immediately to freeze. The thought of his mother, of what she would have said, of the judgment she would have passed on the woman he had chosen, of eventually living with the two women, and of the possible decision of one of the two against a communal family life always intervened to snuff out his ephemeral passion and reject the women who had been the objects of it, as if an affair had been unhappily consummated and he was left thereby with a sense of relief and liberation. Perhaps, had he shut his eyes, he would have married a woman his mother had chosen; but to his mother he was still so ingenuous, so heedless, so vulnerable to the vicissitudes of the world and the times that she deemed him in no position to take such a perilous step.

Given this character and the conditions in which he lived, he had no friends. Many acquaintances, but no friendships. He had gone through *ginnasio* and *liceo* with Dr. Roscio, for example, but later, when they met again, after their years at the university, one could not say that they were friends. They saw each other at the pharmacy and the club; they chatted; they remembered some episode or person from their school days. Occasionally, he called the doctor to the house for some indisposition or depression of his mother. Roscio would come, examine the old lady, prescribe something; he would stay for a cup of coffee and recall this professor or that fellow student whom he had not heard of since the university and who knows what he was doing or where he lived. The call was never paid for, but every year, at Christmas, Laurana sent the doctor a fine book as a gift, for Roscio was one of those who now and then read a book. But there was no affection between them, only a community of memories and the possibility of talking of some literary or political event with a certain propriety and without disagreeable differences—something that was impossible with others in the town; they were almost all of them Fascists, even those who thought they were Socialists or Communists. Roscio's death, therefore, had been a particular blow to Laurana; he had felt the emptiness and the pain of it, especially after he had seen him dead. Death had covered his face with a pale sulphur, a mask of sulphur that slowly hardened in the spent air, heavy with the scent of flowers and wax and sweat. It was as if Roscio had been attacked by a slow petrifaction, and underneath one sensed his anguished surprise, his anguished effort to break through the crust. On the pharmacist, however, death had conferred a dignity and thoughtful gravity that no one had ever detected in him when alive. And so it is that death, too, has its little ironies.

These elements—the disappearance of a man to whom he had been bound by habit rather than by friendship; his first encounter (although he had seen other dead men and other forms of death) with death in all its fearsome objectivity; the pharmacy door closed and seemingly forever sealed by its black mourning crêpe—these elements had given rise to a state of mind akin to desolation, and to periodic anxieties that Laurana noticed even physically in pauses or accelerations of his pulse. But his curiosity about the reasons for, and the method of, the crime was quite divorced from this frame of mind, or so he believed; his curiosity was purely intellectual, inspired by a kind of punctilio. That is, he was rather like the man in a living room or club who hears one of those stupid puzzles volunteered by the fools who are always eager to propose and, what is worse, to solve them, and who knows it is a futile game and a waste of time, played by futile people with time to waste, yet who feels obliged to solve the problem, and doggedly sets about doing so. What is more, the idea that a solution of this problem might, as they say, bring the culprits to the bar of justice, and thereby serve the ends of justice, never even crossed his mind. He was an educated man, intelligent enough, with decent impulses, and he was respectful of the law; but any sense that he was taking over the police's job, or that he was competing with them in their work, would have filled him with such repugnance that he would have let the matter drop.

Yet here is this reflective, timid, perhaps even uncourageous man playing his perilous card, one evening at the club, when almost no one is absent. They are talking, as every other evening, about the crime. And Laurana, who ordinarily is silent, says, "The letter was made up of words clipped from the *Osservatore Romano*."

The discussion is instantly choked off; a stunned silence follows.

"Look here, look here," Don Luigi Corvaia says presently. His amazement is not over the clue that has just been revealed but over the fact that the person who had revealed it should thereby have exposed himself to cross fire from both sides, police and assassins. Who had ever seen such a thing?

"Really? . . . But, excuse me, how do you know that?" Rosello, the cousin of Roscio's wife, asked.

"I noticed it while the marshal was dictating the report to the pharmacist. If you remember, I went into the pharmacy with them."

"And did you point it out to the marshal?" Pecorilla asked.

"Yes, I told him to examine the letter carefully. He said he would."

"Well, then, we can assume they have," Don Luigi said, both slightly relieved and slightly displeased that the revelation was not, after all, so dangerous for Laurana.

"Strange that the marshal hasn't said anything to me," Rosello said.

"Maybe it was a clue that led nowhere," the postmaster said. And then his face lighted up and he said to Laurana, "So that's why you asked me—"

"No," Laurana cut him short. Meanwhile, Colonel Salvaggio, retired yet always poised to explode the moment aspersions, doubts, or criticisms in any way touched the army, the carabinieri, or the police, had got solemnly to his feet and, bearing down on Rosello, was saying, "Would you care to explain to me why the marshal would have had to say anything to you with regard to this or any other clue?"

"As a relative of one of the victims, for Heaven's sake, simply as a relative," the lawyer explained hastily.

"Ah." The Colonel was appeased. He had believed that Rosello was asserting his right to a report from the marshal on the basis of his political position. Then, not entirely satisfied, he returned to the attack. "I might point out that the marshal cannot reveal what is, in effect, a secret of the investigation under way, not even to a relative of one of the victims. He cannot and he should not. And if he were to, he would fall seriously short, seriously short, I say, of his official duty."

"I know," Rosello said, "I know. But like that, out of friendship—"

"The authorities have no friends!" the Colonel almost shouted.

"But marshals do!" Rosello exploded.

"Marshals are authorities, colonels are authorities, corporals are authorities. . . ." The Colonel seemed to be raving and his head began to shake, both preludes to one of those crises the members of the club knew well.

Rosello stood up, signaled to Laurana that he had something to say to him, and they went out together.

"Crazy old man," he said, once they were outside the club. Then, "What is this story about the *Osservatore Romano?*"

6   Nothing had happened after his revelation at the club. Not that he was expecting
anything. He had wanted to see what effect it would have
on each of those present, but the Colonel's intervention had
ruined that. All he had got out of it was that Rosello had
told him, in confidence, how the investigation was going.
Had Colonel Salvaggio overheard, he would have been apo-
plectic, but basically it added up to very little: suspicions,
still, about the secret love life of the pharmacist.

Even without the results he had hoped for, Laurana had
a feeling that among the members of the club and, more
narrowly, among those who habitually frequented the pharmacy, there was something to be discovered. And that was

one single, hard fact: ordinarily, hunters keep the place where they intend to go for the first day of the season a secret, so that they will arrive first and alone on virgin hunting territory. In town, this was habitual. The secret was carefully kept between whoever was sharing in the excursion —in this instance, Manno and Roscio. Rarely was it communicated to a third party, and then only under the seal of silence. Indeed, it often happened that a man would intentionally confide false information. So no one, even had he had a confidential tip from either Manno or Roscio, could have been sure that it was not, as was quite usual, a false clue. Unless it was a question of a friend, of course—a very good friend and, furthermore, a friend who was not a hunter. To a serious, reliable, tested friend who was not infected by a passion for the hunt, probably one of the two men would have revealed where they were going for the opening day of the season.

· Accompanying his mother to call on the widow of the pharmacist and the widow of the doctor, Laurana had the opportunity to make a little check. He asked the same question of both: "Did your husband tell you which area they had decided on for the opening day of the season?"

"Just as he was leaving, he told me that perhaps they would go in the direction of Cannatello," Signora Manno replied. Laurana made mental note of that "perhaps"; it seemed to him to bespeak the reticence of the pharmacist in revealing the secret even to his wife, and only when he was about to leave.

"Had he spoken to you about the letter?"

"No, he hadn't told me anything."

"He didn't want you to worry."

"Quite." The widow's voice was hard, and tinged with irony.

"And then he believed it was a joke, as we all did."

"A joke," the widow sighed. "A joke that has cost him his life and me my reputation."

"His life, yes, unfortunately. . . . But you—come, now, what have you to do with it?"

"What have I to do with it? You haven't heard the shameful things people are saying?"

"Chatter," said the old Signora Laurana. "Chatter that no one with any charity or good sense can pay any mind to." And then, not even she being excessively endowed with the spirit of charity, "But surely your husband, blessed soul, never gave you cause for the slightest suspicion?"

"Never, Signora, never. . . . They put it into the maid's mouth, that story about a jealous scene I am supposed to have made my husband over that—that—well, that girl, the poor thing, who used to come to the pharmacy because she had to. . . . And my maid! If you could see how stupid she is. And ignorant! Why, she trembles just to hear the carabinieri mentioned. . . . They made her say what they wanted her to say. And those Roscios, and the Rosellos . . . Why, even that saintly man, even the Dean . . . They immediately started saying that the doctor, peace be on his soul, died because of my husband's vices. As if we didn't all know each other here, as if we didn't know everyone, know what kind of person he is, what he does, if he gambles, if he steals, if he"—she clapped a hand to her mouth to smother other and more burning possibilities. Then, with calculated malice, she said with a sigh, "That poor Dr. Roscio, what a family he got mixed up with!"

"But I don't think—" Laurana began.

"We all know each other, believe me," Signora Manno interrupted. "You, as everyone knows, are a man who is busy with his studies and his books"—this said almost scornfully—"and you have no time to bother about certain things, whereas we"—she turned to Signora Laurana for confirmation—"we know."

"Yes," the old woman admitted, "we know."

"And then I was a schoolmate of Luisa, Roscio's wife. What a creature she was!"

That creature, on whose score the widow Manno had evoked memories of petty schoolgirl malice and hinted about some nun who had adored her—that creature Laurana now had seated before him in a light subdued by heavy drawn curtains, as is proper in a house of bereavement. The tokens of mourning were everywhere to be seen; even the mirrors were draped in black. But what bespoke loss most eloquently was Roscio's portrait enlarged to life size by a photographer in the county seat, and lugubriously retouched and funeralized with a black suit and black tie (in the social and aesthetic concept of the photographer, by the very fact of their death all the dead whom he enlarged were obliged to conform to mourning protocol), a bitter twist to the mouth, a weary, imploring glance; in the light of the little lamp standing before it, it looked like a strolling player made up to play a ghost.

"No, he never told me," Luisa Roscio had replied to the question did she know where her husband would be going to hunt. "Because, to tell the truth, I didn't look on his passion for hunting too warmly. No more than I liked the companion he'd chosen. Not that I *knew* anything, good Heavens! Maybe it was a presentiment, one of those impressions. . . . And an evil fate has proved me right, unfortunately." With a grief-laden sigh, almost a groan, she raised her handkerchief to her eyes.

"It was the hand of destiny. And what can we do against destiny?" old Signora Laurana comforted her.

"Destiny, ah, yes. . . . But what do you ask of me? When I think how happy, how contented we were, with never the slightest worry, the slightest shadow—then, may God forgive me, I feel desperate, utterly desperate." She threw back her head with a small, silent cry.

"No, no, no," the old woman said, gently disapproving. "Not desperate. You must submit to God's will, offer your grief to God."

"To the Heart of Jesus. That's what Uncle—the Dean—tells me. You see what a beautiful painting of the Heart of Jesus he brought me?" She pointed behind the old lady. The Signora turned and shifted her chair, almost as if until then she had been inadvertently rude, and, by way of greeting, blew a kiss toward the picture, saying, "Sacred Heart of Jesus." Then, "Beautiful, yes, really beautiful. What expression in the eyes!"

"They are a comfort," Signora Luisa admitted.

"You see, then, the comfort of the Lord is with you," the old woman said, in a tone of gentle triumph. "And there are other comforts, other hopes that you have, that you will have always. There is the child. You must think of the child."

"I do. If I did not have her to think about, believe me, I don't know what foolish thing I might do."

"The child"—hesitating—"does she know?"

"She knows nothing, poor little thing, nothing. We told her that Papa went away on a trip and that he will be back."

"But when she sees you dressed in black, doesn't she ask why, doesn't she want to know?"

"No. On the contrary, she told me I'm prettier when I wear black, that I should always dress like this." With her right hand, she lifted the black-bordered handkerchief to her face and broke into almost uncontrolled weeping; with her left hand, she pulled down the hem of her skirt which, as Laurana watched, slipped back up above the knee. "And that is how it will be always," she sobbed. "Always dressed in black, always. . . ."

The child's right, Laurana thought. A beautiful woman, and black became her marvelously. A beautiful body, slender, rounded, with a suggestion of indolence, of abandon, of languor, even when she held herself most tense. The face was full—not the fullness of a woman who has passed thirty but rather of a girl—and glowing, the eyes chestnut, almost golden, the teeth white and perfect between heavy lips. I wish I could see her smile, he thought, but he despaired of any such miracle in the circumstances, what with the turn his mother was giving to the conversation. And yet it did happen, when they came to speak of the pharmacist and the distractions everyone now attributed to him. "I don't say he might not have had his own good reasons. Poor Lucia Spanò was never what you would call a beauty. We went to boarding school together, and she was the same then. Even homelier, maybe." She smiled; then her face darkened again as she said, "But what had my husband to do with it?" And a fresh flood of tears fell into the handkerchief.

7   One corollary of all the detective novels to which a goodly share of mankind repairs for refreshment specifies that a crime present its investigators with a picture, the material and, so to speak, stylistic elements of which, if meticulously assembled and analyzed, permit a sure solution. In actuality, however, the situation is different. The coefficients of impunity and error are high not because, or not only or not always because, the investigators are men of small intelligence but because the clues a crime offers are usually utterly inadequate. A crime, that is to say, which is planned or committed by people who have every interest in working to keep the impunity coefficient high.

The factors that lead to the solution of seemingly mysterious or gratuitous crimes are what may be called the professional stool pigeon, the anonymous informer, and chance. And to a degree—but only to a degree—the acuteness of the investigators.

For Professor Laurana, the case broke in September, in Palermo. He had been in the city for several days, supervising *liceo* examinations. In the restaurant he frequented regularly, he met an old school friend whom he had not seen for a long time but whose political rise he had followed from a distance. A Communist: local secretary of the Party in a small town in the Madonie Mountains; then regional deputy, then national deputy. They reminisced about their student days, naturally, and when their talk touched on poor Roscio, the deputy said, "It shocked me terribly— the news of his death, I mean. He'd been in to see me just two or three weeks before. I hadn't seen him for at least ten years. He came up to Rome to talk to me. I recognized him immediately. He hadn't changed, whereas you and I —well, perhaps a little. . . . It occurred to me that his death might be connected somehow with his having come to see me in Rome, but then I read that the investigation showed he had died simply because he happened to be with someone or other who had seduced a girl, I don't just remember now. . . . And do you know why he'd come to see me? To ask whether I would be willing to denounce on the floor of Parliament and in our Party papers and at Party meetings a prominent person in your town. Someone, he said, who held the whole province in the palm of his hand,

who made men and unmade them, stole, bribed, swin-
dled. . . ."

"A man from our town? Really?"

"Now that I think back, I don't believe he said in so
many words that it was someone from town. Maybe he
gave me to understand that, or I just got that impression."

"A prominent person who holds the whole province in
the palm of his hand?"

"Yes, that I remember very well. Those were his exact
words. Naturally, I told him I would be more than happy
to break the story, to expose the man, but that obviously I
needed some documentation, some proof. He told me he
had a whole dossier available and would bring it to me. But
then he never came back."

"Naturally."

"Yes, naturally, seeing that he was no longer alive."

"No, I didn't mean to joke. I was thinking, your suspicion of there being a connection between his trip to Rome
and his death. . . . I do remember that he wasn't around
for several days. Then he said he'd been to Palermo to see
his father. But it seems almost impossible. Roscio wanting
to denounce someone, I mean, with a dossier in his possession. Are you positive it was Roscio?"

"Good Lord," the deputy said. "I recognized him right
away, I tell you. He hadn't changed a bit."

"It's true, he hadn't changed. . . . He didn't give you
the name of the person he wanted to expose?"

"No, absolutely not."

"He didn't give you even a vague indication, some hint?"

"Nothing. Actually, I insisted he tell me something more, but he said it was such a delicate, such a personal matter—"

"Personal?"

"Personal, yes. With the documentation in hand, he said, he would tell me everything—or nothing. And I admit, when I heard him say he had still to decide whether to tell me everything or nothing, I felt a little uneasy. I got the impression that the documents, and his having come to see me, had something to do with blackmail of some sort. If the business, whatever it was, were to go well, then nothing; and if it went badly, then back to me with the dossier."

"No, he wasn't a man to go in for blackmail. Absolutely not."

"Well, how do you interpret an attitude like that?"

"I don't know. It's very strange. It's almost unbelievable."

"But, excuse me for saying this, isn't it also a little strange that you can't conceive of his wanting to strike at someone, and can't imagine whom or why? You were close to him, after all; you knew him well. Doesn't it seem to you that there's something equivocal about it all?"

"I wasn't so close to him. And as a person, he was rather withdrawn; he never confided in anyone. So we never talked about private, intimate things. We talked about books, politics."

"What did he think about politics?"

"He thought political action that failed to take moral principles into account—"

"Moral principles!" The deputy snorted.

"I rather agree with him."

"Really?"

"That doesn't prevent my voting for the Communist Party."

"Good, good," the deputy said approvingly.

"But with considerable uneasiness and concern."

"And why is that?" the deputy asked, with an indulgently amused glance that threatened immediate demolition of any argument Laurana might put forward.

"Let's let that go. You'll never manage to persuade me to vote against it."

"Against what?"

"Against the Communist Party."

"That's good," the deputy said, laughing.

"Not entirely. It's a protest vote," Laurana said seriously, and he went back to the subject of Roscio, who might possibly have voted Communist, although he would have been careful not to say so. "Out of respect for his relatives—his wife's relatives, that is. They're all active politically, the Dean first and foremost."

"The Dean?"

"Yes, Dean Rosello, the wife's uncle. So, out of respect or to avoid family quarrels, perhaps, Roscio avoided taking definite positions. However, I must say that toward the last he had become more severe, more bitter, in his judgments about politicians and political matters generally. About the administration's policies, let's say."

"Maybe they whisked some plum, some appointment, away from him."

"I don't believe so. . . . You see, he was different from what you, at this point, could imagine him. He loved his work, he loved the town, the evenings at the club or the pharmacy, and hunting and dogs. I think he loved his wife very much, and he adored their little girl."

"What's that got to do with it? He could love money, too, have ambitions to be something or other."

"Money he had. And he had no ambitions. A man who has chosen of his own free will to live in a small city, who has no intention of leaving it—what ambitions can he have left?"

"The old-fashioned country doctor, in other words. The type that used to live on what he had, never charged for his calls, and sometimes left his poor patients money for the medicine."

"Something like that. And yet he earned well enough. He had the reputation of being a good doctor, and lots of people came to his office from other towns nearby to be taken care of by him. And then there was the name—Roscio. Old Professor Roscio . . . By the bye, I think I'll go call on him."

"But in a word: Do you think Roscio's death can really be linked to his being against some well-known unknown townsman?"

"No. Quite the contrary. All appearances indicate that Roscio is dead today because incautiously—I say incautiously, because he knew about the threat—he went along with Manno. These are the indications."

"Poor Roscio," the deputy said.

8   Old Dr. Roscio, whose fame as an eye
specialist still survived in western Sicily and
was indeed assuming the proportions of myth, had given
up his university chair and active practice some twenty years
earlier. He was now over ninety and, whether because of
the irony of fate or so that he might better incarnate the
myth of the man who defied Nature by restoring sight to
the blind and therefore had his own vision impaired by
Nature, the professor was afflicted by almost total blind-
ness. He lived in Palermo with a son who was probably an
equally gifted eye specialist but who, in the light of most
people's prejudices, lived on the credit of his father's name.
Laurana telephoned to announce his visit for whatever

day and hour would be most convenient for the professor. The professor, when the maid went to tell him of the call, came to the phone himself. Laurana should come directly, he said. Not that he had managed to remember, from the references Laurana gave him, who this old friend of his son was; in the dark solitude where he now lived, he was simply greedy for company.

It was five o'clock in the afternoon. The professor was out on the terrace, sitting in an armchair, with a gramophone beside him from which issued the now stentorian, now tremulous, now whispering voice of a famous actor who was reciting Canto XXX of the "Inferno."

"You see what I am reduced to?" the professor said, holding out his hand. "I must listen to *him* recite the *Divine Comedy*." He spoke as if the actor were present, and as if he had other and more personal reasons for despising the actor. "I'd rather my nephew read to me—he's twelve—or the maid or the doorman, but they have other things to do."

Beyond the terrace balustrade, Palermo shimmered under the wind veils of the sirocco. "Beautiful view," the professor said, and with assurance he pointed: "San Giovanni degli Eremiti, Palazzo d'Orleans, Palazzo Reale." He smiled. "When we came to live in this house, ten years ago, I saw a little more. Now I just detect light, like a faraway white flame. Luckily, there is so much light in Palermo. . . . But that's enough of these personal miseries. So you were a school friend of my poor son?"

"In grammar school and *liceo*. Then he went on into medicine and I took up literature."

"Literature. And so you teach, yes?"

"Yes. Italian language and history."

"Do you know, I'm sorry now that I didn't become a professor of literature. At least I'd have known the *Divine
Comedy* by heart."

It's a fixation, Laurana thought. Aloud, he said, "But in
your life you have done much more than read and expound
the *Divine Comedy.*"

"Do you believe what I did makes more sense than what
you do?"

"No. I mean that what I do thousands of other people
can do. But what you did, very few people can do—perhaps
ten, twenty people in the world."

"Nonsense," the old man said, and he seemed to doze
off. Then, suddenly, he asked, "My son . . . how was he
toward the end?"

"How was he?"

"Did he seem worried, I mean. Restless, nervous?"

"He didn't seem so to me. But yesterday, as I was talking
with someone who had met him in Rome, I remembered
that he really did seem a little different recently—in some
ways, at least. But how is it that you ask me that?"

"Because he seemed a little different to me, too. . . .
Someone who had met him in Rome, you say?"

"Yes, in Rome. Two or three weeks before the accident
happened."

"Strange. . . . This person isn't mistaken, by any chance?"

"He's not mistaken. He's a friend, an old fellow student.
A deputy now, a Communist. Your son had gone to Rome
specifically to meet him."

"To meet him? That's strange, that really is strange. . . .

I don't believe he would have had any favor to ask. The Communists are in a position to do favors, too, in a way, but it's always easier to get the other people"—he gestured toward the Palazzo d'Orleans, the seat of the regional Christian Democrat administration. "And my son had some of them in his own family—rather powerful people, they tell me."

"It wasn't exactly a favor he was after. He wanted our friend to speak in Parliament and expose abuses and thefts that have been committed by some prominent person."

"My son?" the old man was dumfounded.

"Yes. I was surprised, too."

"Certainly he had changed," the old man said reflectively, almost as if to himself. "He had changed. I don't know exactly, I can't remember exactly when I first noticed a kind of weariness in him, a kind of—estrangement. And a severity in passing judgment that made me think of his mother. Eh, my wife wasted no love on her neighbor. . . . Maybe it would be fairer to say that she didn't understand other people, that no one had ever been able to make her understand. Least of all me. . . . What were we talking about?"

"Your son."

"Yes, about my son . . . He was intelligent, but it was a quiet, slow intelligence. And he was very honest. With a deep attachment to the land, which he inherited from his mother, maybe. But that's all, because his grandfather—my wife's father—lived in the country like some wild animal, and my wife, too; while my son, on the other hand, was a cultivated man, I believe. . . . As a boy, and as a man, he

was what you call a simple person, but actually that kind of
person is devilishly complex. That's why I never liked his
getting mixed up with a Catholic family through his marriage. 'Catholic' in a manner of speaking, I mean. Never
knew a true Catholic around here in my whole life, and I'm
going on ninety-two. In the course of a lifetime some people
will have eaten half a salma's worth of wheat in the form
of Communion wafers, and they're the same people who
are always ready to put their hand in another man's pocket
or push a dying man's teeth in or kick a healthy man in
the groin. . . . You know my daughter-in-law, her relatives?"

"Not intimately."

"Don't know them at all myself. Met my daughter-in-law
a few times, and that uncle of hers once—the rector or dean
or whatever the devil he is."

"Dean."

"A very soft-spoken man. Wanted to convert me. He was
only passing through town, luckily, or one day he'd have
fetched me the Sacrament as a surprise. He didn't understand at all that I am a religious man. . . . My daughter-in-
law is very beautiful, isn't she?"

"Very beautiful."

"Or perhaps simply very much a woman. . . . The kind
that when I was young used to be called bed-worthy"—
this with the detachment of a man who knows whereof he
speaks, almost as if he were not referring to his dead son's
wife, and his hands sketched a recumbent body—"but I
believe the expression's no longer in use. Women have lost
their mystery, the physical and the spiritual mystery both.

And do you know what I think? I think that today the Catholic Church is racking up its greatest victory: at long last, men hate women. Never before did the Church manage that, not even in the darkest dark ages. But today it has. A theologian might say that it is a trick of Providence. Man believed that he was traveling the highway toward freedom even in the matter of eroticism, but instead he's as shackled by religious superstitions as ever."

"Perhaps, yes. . . . Although it seems to me that today, in a world we call Christian, the body of woman has been emphasized—has been exposed—as never before. And the same function of appeal, of fascination, that advertising assigns to women—"

"You've used a word that says it all in a nutshell. 'Exposed.' The body of woman is exposed. Exposed the way once upon a time we used to expose the bodies of hanged men. . . . Justice has been done, in a word. But here I am, talking too much. I'd better rest a little."

Laurana took this as a dismissal, and hastily got to his feet.

"Please don't go," the old man said, alarmed that the rare opportunity for conversation might escape him so fast. Again he seemed to doze off, to slip into sleep, turning toward Laurana the fine, medallion-like profile that generations of students would see on a bronze bas-relief in the entrance hall of the university, with one of those inscriptions underneath that, if ever they are read, make people laugh. "He'll slip into death like that," Laurana thought, and sat watching him with some anxiety until the old man, still motionless, spoke out as if he were developing a thought that had been absorbing him: "Some things, some facts, are better left where they are, kept in the dark. . . . There's a proverb, a maxim, that runs, 'The dead man is dead; let's give a hand to the living.' Now, you say that to a man from the North, and he visualizes the scene of an accident with one dead and one injured man; it's reasonable to let the dead man be and to set about saving the injured man. But a Sicilian visualizes a murdered man and his murderer, and the living man who's to be helped is the murderer. What a dead man means to a Sicilian—well, maybe Lawrence understood that; he helped drive Eros into a cul-de-sac. A dead man is a ridiculous spirit in purgatory, a little worm with human features writhing on a hot brick. But when the dead man is our own flesh and blood, then, of course, we must do everything to send the live man—the murderer, that is— to join him forthwith in hell-fire. . . . I'm not a Sicilian to that extent. I've never had any inclination to help the living—the murderers, that is—and I've always thought jails were a more solid purgatory. . . . But there is something about my son's death that makes me think about the living, makes me a little concerned for the living—"

"The murderers, you mean?"

"No, not the living men who personally, physically killed him. The living who alienated him from life, who brought him to a point where he saw certain things in life and did others. . . . Anyone who's chanced to reach my age is inclined to think of death as an act of will; in my case, a small act of will. At some point, I'll get tired of hearing that voice"—he gestured toward the gramophone—"and the noise of the city and the maid who's been singing the same song about the same tear-stained cheek for six months and my daughter-in-law who's been inquiring every morning for ten years about my health with the scantily disguised hope of hearing that I've come to the final amen. And then I'll decide to die—the way you hang up the phone when you've got a bore or a fool at the other end of the line. But I want to say this: certain experiences—an injury, a thought, a state of mind—can make a man look on death as a mere formality. And in that case, if someone may be said to be responsible, we must look among the people who were closest to him. In the case of my son, you could start with me, for a father is always guilty, always. . . ." His eyes seemed lost in the far reaches of the past, of memory. "As you see, I am also one of the living who must be helped."

Laurana suspected there might be a kind of double meaning in this, or perhaps it was only a dim, painful intuition. He asked, "Are you thinking of something specific?"

"Oh, nothing specific. I'm thinking of the living. And you?"

"I don't know," Laurana said.

Silence fell between them. Laurana got up to take his leave. The old man held out a hand. "It's a problem," he said, and he was perhaps alluding to the crime, perhaps to life.

9   He went back home at the end of
September. There was nothing new, Rosello
informed him immediately, drawing him to one side at the
club so that the redoubtable Colonel would not overhear.
It was Laurana who had news for the lawyer: his meeting
with the deputy, the story of the documents Roscio had
promised the politician provided he would launch the exposé.

Rosello was thunderstruck. He listened to the story, saying over and over "Think of that!" And then he recapitu-
lated it himself, probing, trying to recall some sign, some
word of Roscio's to which the unbelievable story could be
attached.

"I supposed you would know something about it," Laurana said.

"Know something! I'm flabbergasted."

"Perhaps the person he was about to attack was a man from your Party. Maybe he wanted to avoid your becoming involved and persuading him not to go ahead. He was stubborn, but in some ways he was very malleable. If you'd known, you would have intervened, pressured him, tried to smooth things over. Certainly you couldn't have been indifferent when a man of your Party—and by extension the Party itself—was threatened."

"When it is a matter of the family, of any member of the family, there is no party that could weigh in the balance. If he had turned to me, he'd have had all the satisfaction he wanted."

"But maybe that's exactly what he did not want. Perhaps he didn't want you to compromise your position in the Party over something that concerned him. He did say, in fact, that it had to do with a delicate and personal matter."

"Delicate and personal . . . Are you sure he mentioned no names? Didn't he give some indication that would identify this prominent person? Even if only approximately?"

"Nothing."

"You know what? I'm going to telephone my cousin, and we'll see her together. He must have said something to his wife. Come with me."

They went to the telephone, and Rosello spoke to his cousin: he was with Professor Laurana, who had heard certain things, quite incredible things, things that perhaps only she could explain, and would they be disturbing her if they came to see her for a moment at such a possibly inconvenient hour?

"Let's go," Rosello said, as he hung up.

The Signora was waiting, tremulous with anxiety to know what the professor had to tell. She was astounded to hear of her husband's trip to Rome. Looking at her cousin, she said, "He must have gone there when he said he was going to Palermo, two or three weeks before the accident," but to the rest she had nothing to say. Yes, perhaps her husband had been a little preoccupied recently, had little to say, often suffered from headaches.

"His father, too—old Professor Roscio—told me that recently his son had seemed to him changed."

"You saw my father-in-law?"

"Formidable old man," Rosello said.

"Yes, I went to call on him. He has his little oddities, but he is lucid, even merciless, I'd say."

"He has no religion," the Signora said. "What can you expect of a man who has no religion?"

"Intellectually merciless, I meant. As to religion, I think he is religious."

"No, he is not," Rosello said. "He is an atheist, of the ironclad breed that doesn't give in even at death's door."

"Neither do I believe he is an atheist," Laurana said.

"He's anticlerical," the Signora said. "We went to visit him once, my husband, my uncle—the Dean—and I. The things he said! They gave me the shivers, believe me." She hugged her beautiful bare arms, as if assailed still by those shivers.

"What did he say?"

"Things I can't repeat, things such as I'd never heard in my life. And there poor Uncle sat, holding his silver Crucifix and talking to him about forgiveness and love."

"He told me, actually, that the Dean is a very gentle man."

"Well he might say so," the Signora said.

"The Dean is a saint," Rosello chimed in.

"No, you can't say that, you must not say that," the Signora corrected him. "The saints are not made by us, we cannot make them. . . . Uncle has—this much you can say —he has such goodness of heart that it makes one think of saintliness."

"Your husband," Laurana said, "resembled his father physically a great deal, and also a little in his way of thinking."

"Resembled that lost old man? For mercy's sake! My husband had great respect for the Dean, and for the Church, too. He used to go with me to Mass every Sunday. He observed Friday. And never did he say a scornful or skeptical word about religious things. And much as I loved him, do you believe I would have married him if I'd suspected, even just suspected, that he thought as his father does?"

"To tell the truth," Rosello said, "he was a hard man to understand. What he might have thought about religion or about politics I don't believe even you, his wife, can say definitely."

"Certainly he was respectful," the Signora retrenched.

"That, yes, respectful. But from what Laurana has just told us, it's clear that he was a closed person, that he did not confide his ideas or plans even in you."

"That is true." The Signora sighed. And to Laurana: "But his father—he didn't say anything even to his father?"

"Nothing."

"And to the deputy he said that it had to do with something delicate and personal?"

"Yes."

"And he promised him documents?"

"A whole dossier."

"Listen," Rosello proposed to his cousin, "can't we just glance through his drawers, his papers?"

"I want everything to remain the way he left it. I wouldn't have the heart to touch anything."

"But this is a question of setting our minds at rest. And then—oh, I don't know, but if someone had wronged him, out of respect for his memory, the affection I had for him, I can go further, get to the bottom of whatever—"

"You're right," the Signora said, and she stood up. Erect, bosom swelling, arms bare to the heavily tufted armpits, winged by a scent in which a more expert nose (and a less ardent nature) would have distinguished between Balenciaga and sweat, she overwhelmed the professor, who for a moment saw in her the Victory of Samothrace sweeping up the stairway of the Louvre.

She led them to the study, a rather dark room, or so it seemed in the light that, falling on the desk, left the plain book-laden shelves in the shadow. A book lay open on the desk. "He was reading it," the Signora said. Marking the place with two fingers, Rosello closed it and read the title: "*Letters to Madame Z.*"

"What kind of stuff is it?" he asked Laurana.

"Very interesting. By a Pole."

"He read so much," the Signora said.

With more care than he had shown in picking up the book, Rosello laid it back, open, on the desk. "Let's have a look at the desk first," he said. He pulled out the top drawer.

Laurana leaned over the open book, and the words leaped out at him from the page: "Only the action that affects the organization of a system exposes men to the harsh light of the law." Taking the whole page in at a glance, as if he were unfurling a screen rather than reading the lines, he recognized the context; it was where the writer speaks of Camus and *The Stranger*. The organization of a system! he thought. And what system existed here? Had there ever been, would there ever be one? To be strangers in truth or in guilt, or in truth and guilt together, is a luxury that one can allow oneself only when there is an ordered system. Unless one chose to consider what poor Roscio disappeared in to be a system. In which case, man is more of a stranger in the role of executioner than in that of victim; more with the truth if he operates the guillotine and less so if he kneels under it.

The Signora had lent her hand to the search; she was squatting before the bottom drawer of the desk, framed in the square formed by the play of light and shadow, nakedly female, her face mysteriously concealed beneath the dark mass of her hair. Laurana's thoughts dissolved in the black sun of desire.

The Signora shut the drawer and rose lightly to her feet, like a dancer. "Nothing," she said; she showed no disappointment, rather as if she had undertaken the search only to satisfy her cousin. "Nothing," Rosello said also and in the same tone of voice, putting the last folder of papers in order.

"There could be, I don't know, a safe-deposit box at the bank," Laurana said.

"I was thinking of that, too," Rosello said, "and tomorrow I'll see what I can find out."

"Impossible. He knew that here no one touched his things, his books and papers, not even I. He was quite meticulous," the Signora said; her inflection gave one to understand that meticulous she was not.

"Certainly there is something mysterious about all this," Rosello said.

"But do you think that this story of the Communist deputy and the documents has anything to do with his death?" she asked.

"Not in my wildest dreams." He turned to Laurana. "What do you say?"

"Who can say?"

"Oh!" It was almost a cry. "Do you think—"

"No, I don't. It's just that when things have reached this point, with the police insisting on a blind alley—the pharmacist's nonexistent love affairs, I mean—all hypotheses are good."

"And the letter? The threatening letter the pharmacist received? How do you account for the letter?" Rosello asked.

"Yes, what about the letter?" the Signora urged.

"The letter," Laurana said, "I ascribe to the cleverness of the murderers. The pharmacist was the false target; he was the screen."

"Do you really believe that?" the Signora asked, stunned, devastated.

"No, I don't believe it."

The woman seemed relieved. Laurana thought, She's latched onto the idea that her husband died because of the pharmacist, and she thinks any other hypothesis is an offense to his memory, to his cult. He reproached himself for having upset her with a hypothesis of his that, in point of fact, he did not consider totally improbable.

10   "A prominent person who bribes, swindles, steals. . . . Who comes to mind?"

"Here in town?"

"Maybe in town, maybe in the vicinity, maybe in the province."

"You're asking me a hard question," the rector of Sant'-Anna said. "Because if we confine ourselves to town, any newborn infant knows the answer. But if we branch out into the immediate vicinity, much less the province, the prospect is one to make the head spin. Chaos."

"Then let's stick to town," Laurana said.

"Rosello. Rosello, the lawyer."

"Impossible."

"What's impossible?"

"For him to be the person."

"Impossible for him to be a man who bribes, steals, swindles? In that case, forgive my saying so, but I must tell you that none are so blind as those who won't see."

"No, no. . . . What I mean is, it's impossible that the person . . . the person I've been talking with would have meant him. Out of the question."

"And who is this person you've been talking with?"

"I can't mention his name." Laurana flushed, and he avoided the rector's eyes, which had suddenly sharpened.

"My dear professor, this person did not give you the name of the prominent figure; he did not give you the name of the town. He gave you some details that, believe me, would describe—excluding those honorable gentlemen who have been picked up already and are currently residing in our nation's jails—details that would describe, what can I say, a hundred thousand individuals, give or take a few. And from this army you expect to draw your man, your prominent person?" He smiled indulgently, pityingly.

"To tell the truth, I had supposed that the person whose name I can't mention was referring to someone here in town. But if you tell me there's only Rosello—"

"Rosello is the biggest, the one who comes to mind first. And he's the only one who, properly speaking, belongs to the category of prominent people. Then there are the little fellows. One can include even me in the bouquet of little fellows."

"Certainly not," Laurana protested, without conviction.

"Oh yes, and perhaps rightly so. But, I say again, Rosello

is the biggest. Do you have any real notion of what Rosello is? His chicanery, I mean, his sources of income, his public and hidden power? Because it's a simple matter to know what he is in human terms. An idiot who is not without guile. To capture and keep a post—a well-paid one, naturally —he would walk over anyone's dead body. Except his uncle's—the Dean's—of course."

"I know what kind of man he is, but I don't know exactly how powerful he is. No doubt you are better informed than I."

"I am, you had better believe I am! . . . Well, Rosello is on the board of directors of Furaris, five hundred thousand lire a month. He is legal consultant for Furaris, a couple of million lire a year. He is a director of the Trinacria Bank, another couple of million. He is a member of the management committee of Vesceris, five hundred thousand lire a month. He is president of a corporation—financed by Furaris and Trinacria—which was set up to quarry rare marble and operates, as everyone knows, in an area where a chip of rare marble would never be found even if you were to carry it there, because it would immediately sink into the sand. He is a provincial councilor, and this is one function that, from a financial point of view, represents a total loss, since the vouchers he gets for attending meetings barely cover the tips to the Council ushers. But the *prestige* . . . You know that in the Provincial Council it was he who swung the Council members from his own Party away from an alliance with the Fascists to an alliance with the Socialists? That was one of the very first political deals of its kind in Italy. The result is, he stands in well with the Socialists, and he'll do the same with the Communists if ever his Party seems likely to make another move to the Left and he manages to be one jump ahead. I can tell you, as a matter of fact, that the Communists around here have got a hopeful eye on him already. . . . And now we come to his personal business interests, which I know about only in part: building sites in the county seat and also, they say, in Palermo; control of a couple of construction firms; a printing plant that works to capacity on jobs for the government and for private organizations; a trucking company. . . . Then there are more obscure activities but here, even out of plain, disinterested curiosity, it is dangerous to nose about. I can say this much: if someone were to tell me that the white-slave traffic is in his hands, I would believe it without an oath."

"I would never have believed it," Laurana said.

"Naturally not. But you know? I read once in some book or other on philosophy—a discussion of relativism, it was—that the fact that we, with the naked eye, do not see the feet of the worms in the cheese is no reason to believe that the worms do not see them. . . . I am a worm in the same cheese and I see the other worms' feet."

"Very funny."

"Not so very," the rector said. And, with a grimace of disgust: "The worms we have with us always."

The bitterness of the comment brought Laurana to the brink of confiding in the rector. What if he were to tell him all he knew about the crime and Roscio? An intelligent, keen man, of broad and liberal experience—who knows, he might be able to find the key to the problem. But, on second thought, the rector talked too much, and he loved to pass for being an emancipated man, unprejudiced and corrupt. Furthermore, it was common knowledge that he entertained a profound aversion for the Dean; were he to learn something that cast the slightest reflection on the Dean's family, he would not have refrained from embroidering and spreading the story. An unconscious repugnance for the wayward priest also played a role in Laurana's diffidence, although consciously he contended that there was no such thing as a good priest; it was the same distaste that his mother did not hide for the rector of Sant'Anna, whose "indecent" behavior contrasted so sharply, she used to say, with the chaste comportment of the Dean.

"Leaving Rosello aside, who else is there in the province who has, let's say, the same qualifications?"

"Let me think," the rector said. Then he asked, "Should we exclude deputies and senators?"

"Let's exclude them."

"Well, then, Commendatore Fedeli, Dr. Jacopitto, several lawyers—Lavina, Anfosso, Evangelista, Boiano—Professor Camerlato, and Macomer, that's another lawyer—"

"An insoluble problem, or at least so it seems."

"Eh, insoluble, yes. I told you so. There are too, too many of them—more than someone who is not in the cheese himself can readily believe. But what—well, excuse me, what concern is it of yours to solve this problem?"

"Curiosity, simple curiosity. . . . I met a fellow on the train, and he was telling me about someone from around here who was making money, lots of money, in various illegal ways." From the time he had begun to busy himself about the crime, Laurana lied with some facility; it troubled him a bit, as if he had discovered a hidden proclivity.

"Oh, well. . . ." The rector dismissed a minor matter with a wave of the hand. But he did not appear entirely convinced.

"I'm sorry to have wasted so much of your time," Laurana said.

"I was reading the Casanova memoirs, the unexpurgated text. In French," he added, with a touch of satisfaction.

"I haven't read them yet," Laurana said.

"It's not that there are so many differences from the edition we know. A little less florid, perhaps. . . . I was thinking that if one considers the memoirs as a kind of erotic manual, the most interesting, the truest thing is this: that it is easier to seduce two or three women together than to seduce one alone."

"Is that so?" the professor said, marveling.

"A fact, I assure you," the rector said, placing his hand over his heart.

11 Laurana remembered very clearly: up
until the eve of the crime, Roscio and Ro-
sello had always greeted each other in public, chatted together. Not that they exhibited the closeness of relatives or
the cordiality of friends. But then Roscio maintained with
everyone, even with the pharmacist who was his constant
hunting companion, a detachment that might seem like
coldness or indifference. His conversation, moreover, was
limited to replies; the more numerous the group, the more
he withdrew into a bemused, remote silence. Only with an
old companion like Laurana, and only if the two of them
were alone or somewhat apart, would he talk more easily.

Presumably, he behaved in the same way with the pharmacist on the long days they spent hunting.

His relationship with his wife's cousin seemed unchanged, even in those last days, although it would have been difficult to detect change in Roscio's laconic manner. All the same, they did talk to each other, and this gainsaid any suspicion that Roscio was setting a trap for his relative. Unless one were to ascribe to him some secret, subtle perfidy; that is, the capacity—which was not rare in those parts—diligently to mask one's animosity toward another person while preparing to strike him down in the vilest fashion. But this hypothesis Laurana was unwilling even to consider.

He had come to the point where there was nothing for him to do but to drop the affair, to give it no more thought. It had been a holiday diversion, and a rather foolish one, at that. Schools were reopening, and he would have to resume the uncomfortable routine of shuttling between home and county seat, for his mother was attached to her home town and house, and firmly rejected any proposal to move to the city. And although he felt rather victimized by his mother's attitude, coming back to town after the school day and living in the big old house where he had been born were pleasures that Laurana would never have given up.

However, the bus schedules were decidedly inconvenient. He had to leave every morning at seven; a half hour later, he arrived in the county seat and had to wander about for half an hour, waiting for school to open, or spend the time in the faculty sitting room or at some café. After his last class, he had to wait until one-thirty to catch the return bus, which meant he got home at two. It was a life he found

increasingly onerous from one year to the next, for in passing the years leave their weight behind them.

The advice that everyone (except his mother) kept re-
peating—that he learn to drive and buy a car—had never
seemed to him compatible with his age, his nerves, or, except where his mother's apprehensions were concerned, his
absent-mindedness. But more weary now, and filled with
lassitude at the prospect of the new school term and another
year of the bus, he decided to try. And if, in the instructor's
opinion, his first efforts to drive should show that his attention or reflexes were inadequate, he would immediately
stop and resignedly return to his old habits, even if they
were a greater burden.

This minor decision was to play the role of Fate in his
life. Not that he had really managed to stop thinking from
one day to the next about the question of Roscio's (and the
pharmacist's) death, but an encounter he had as he was
walking up the steps of the Palazzo di Giustizia, where he
had gone to apply for the certificate of his penal purity (indispensable to qualify as a licensed driver), marked the
emergence of a fresh clue to the problem. Chance, once
again, but this time chance fraught with fatality.

As he climbed the steps of the Palazzo, he was maso-
chistically mulling over the apprehensions typical of any
Italian about to enter the labyrinth of a public office building, especially one that goes by the name of Justice. He
found himself walking toward Rosello, who was coming
down the steps accompanied by two persons, one of whom
Laurana immediately recognized: the Honorable Abello,
considered by his devoted admirers and by his Party to be a

champion of political morality and doctrine. Of that doctrine he had more than once provided evidence by demonstrating that in Saint Augustine, Saint Thomas, and Saint Ignatius, and in each and every other saint who had ever put pen to paper or whose thoughts had been collected by some contemporary, Marxism had been triumphantly vanquished. Vanquishments in any and all fields were the forte of the Honorable Abello.

Rosello seemed pleased at the meeting; it was an opportunity to bring Laurana, who sipped culture, into direct touch with that eternal fountain of culture, the Honorable Abello. He duly presented the young man and, with a "My dear sir," the Deputy absently held out his hand, but he became more attentive when Rosello told him that Laurana, a professor at the classical *liceo*, also devoted himself to literary criticism.

"Literary criticism?" the Deputy said, and he raised an inquisitorial eyebrow. "And what have you written by way of literary criticism?"

"Some short pieces . . . on Quasimodo, Campana . . ."

"Unh-unh, Quasimodo," the Deputy said, abruptly disenchanted.

"You don't like him?"

"Not at all. Sicily today has one great poet, Luciano De Mattia. Do you know him?"

"No."

" 'Attend, Federico, unto my voice/That comes to you on the sea gulls' wings' . . . Never heard that? That's from a poem by De Mattia, a marvelous poem dedicated to Federico II. Look it up, read it."

To rescue a Laurana thus crushed by the Deputy's potent cultivation, Rosello intervened, with a smile that underlined just how friendly and sympathetic was his help: "What on earth brings you to these parts? Do you need something?"

Laurana explained that he had come to get a certificate of his unblemished penal record and why he was requesting it. Meanwhile, with vague curiosity, he was watching the man who accompanied Rosello and the Deputy and who had moved somewhat apart. A political hack of the Deputy or a client of the lawyer? A man from the country, obviously, but the curious thing about his appearance was the contrast between his glasses with thin metal frames, such as Americans of a certain age often wear—Truman for one —and his broad, hard, sunburned features. And perhaps out of uneasiness at feeling himself the object of even this vague, unfocused curiosity, the man reached into his pocket and pulled out a packet, and from the packet he took a cigar.

The Deputy held out his hand again, and his parting "My dear sir" was now marked with scorn rather than absent-mindedness. As he was shaking that hand, Laurana noted the yellow and red of the package the man was slipping back into his pocket. He bade farewell to Rosello and, inadvertently, nodded to the man who had been standing apart.

Twenty minutes later, he rushed from the Palazzo di Giustizia because he had still an hour of teaching at school, and as he was passing a tobacconist's, those colors suddenly flamed in his memory. The impulse was instantaneous: he went into the shop and asked for a packet of Branca cigars.

During the few seconds the tobacconist's hand moved along the shelf until it paused at the pigeonhole of the

Brancas, his heartbeat quickened, and a flood of emotion surged to his head, as with the roulette player following the slow, slow motion of the ball on the wheel. And then the package of Brancas was laid on the counter before him: yellow and red. Laurana's sense of having gambled and won was so burningly intense that he thought, Yellow and red, imitating the croupier's cadenced tone in his mind and perhaps even aloud; quite possibly aloud, for the tobacconist paused a moment to look at him. He paid and left. His hands shook when he opened the package, and as he took out a cigar and lighted it, he unconsciously postponed the pleasure of meditating on the dazzling clue that had come to join with the others he already knew; his mind wandered; there was no yellow on a roulette wheel, he reflected, and in memory's eye he saw again the gaming rooms at Monte Carlo where he had been once with the possessed eyes of Ivan Mosyukin—Mattia Pascal.

When he reached school, the director was already in the hallway to monitor the classroom where the boys had begun to be noisy. "Professor, Professor," he chided blandly.

"I'm sorry," Laurana said as he entered the classroom, the lighted cigar in his hand. He was satisfied, confused, frightened. His pupils greeted the novelty of the cigar with a shout of delight.

12   For all he knew, the man who smoked
Branca cigars could equally well be a hired
ruffian or a college professor from Dallas come to take intellectual suck at the bosom, rich-flowing with culture, of the
Honorable Abello. Only his instinct, which in Laurana as in
every Sicilian was sharpened by long experience and fear,
warned him of danger. Thus the dog sniffing the tracks of
the porcupine feels the sting of the quills even before he
sights him, and howls mournfully.

After a meeting with Rosello that same evening, his presentiment became a certainty.

Even before shaking hands, Rosello asked him, "How did

the Deputy impress you?" He was smiling with self-satis-
faction and pride.

Laurana weighed an ambiguous reply. "He deserves," he
said, "the admiration that he enjoys."

"I am pleased you think that, I am really pleased. He is a
man who strikes sparks, an extraordinary mind. You'll see,
sooner or later they'll make him a Minister."

"Of the Interior?" Laurana was unable to suppress a note
of irony.

"Why Interior?" Rosello asked suspiciously.

"Where would you want to put a man like that? In Tour-
ism?"

"Oh, well, of course, the people up in Rome must understand. They'll have to give him an important ministry, a
key ministry."

"They'll understand," Laurana said firmly.

"Let's hope so. Because it is a real crime that at such a
delicate moment in our political life, in our history, a man
like him is not used for all he's worth."

"But, if I'm not mistaken, he stands rather to the Right.
Perhaps at a moment when the trend is to the Left—"

"The Honorable Abello's Right is more Left than the
Chinese, if you really want to know. What does it mean,
Left, Right? These distinctions mean nothing to him."

"I'm glad to hear it," Laurana said. And then, casually,
"Who was the man with the Deputy?"

"A man from Montalmo, a good—" Abruptly he stiff-
ened, and his eyes grew hard and cold. "Why do you ask?"

"Just out of curiosity. He was an interesting sort of fellow."

"Yes, he is indeed an interesting sort of fellow"—this said
in a voice that was shot through with an obscure mockery
and menace.

A shiver of fear branched along Laurana's nerves. He tried
to turn the talk back to the Deputy. "Does the Honorable
Abello go along completely with the line your Party is following now?" he asked.

"Why not? We have nibbled on the Right for twenty
years, and now it's time to nibble on the Left. Anyhow, it
makes no difference."

"And the Chinese?"

"The Chinese?"

"I mean, since the Deputy stands farther Left than the
Chinese—"

"There you go. You Communists are all alike. You take
one little remark and make a rope out of it to hang a man
with. That was just a manner of speaking, to say that he's
more Left than the Chinese. If you like, I can also tell you
that he's farther Right than Franco. He is an extraordinary
man, a man with such big ideas that these wretched little
matters of Right and Left mean nothing to him, as I told
you. . . . But you must excuse me. We'll have to talk about
it another time. I have things to attend to, I must go home."
He went off, a bit flushed in the face and without shaking
hands.

He came back a half hour later, completely changed; he
was cheerful, cordial, even jocular. But Laurana sensed the
tension, the concern, perhaps the fear that made the lawyer
hover "like a moth," he said to himself, "like a death's-head
moth around a light." He—Rosello—tried to bring the con-

versation around again to that fellow Laurana had asked about, the man from Montalmo: maybe he wasn't from Montalmo, after all; on second thought, perhaps he lived in the county seat. He'd said the man was from Montalmo because once—one of the two times he'd met him—he had seen him in Montalmo; he was a good fellow because the Deputy had always spoken of him as a good fellow, devoted, loyal. . . . And so on, until he singed his wings, Rosello did, in the flame of Laurana's suspicion. It was pitiful to watch.

The next afternoon, Laurana took the bus to Montalmo. An old fellow-student from the university lived there, and had invited him repeatedly to make the trip to see some recent excavations that had turned up very interesting things from the classical period in Sicily.

It was a beautiful town, open and harmonious, straight streets radiating from an unspoiled baroque piazza. His friend lived on the square, in a great palazzo as dark within as it was light without, for its compact sandstone seemed to have caught and imprisoned the sun.

His friend was not at home; he had, in fact, gone out to the diggings, of which he was honorary inspector. An elderly maid told Laurana this through a mere crack in the door that she quite evidently wished to close promptly in his face. But from within the house, as though across a long vista of open doors, came a voice that asked imperiously, "Who is it?" Still holding the door ajar, the maid turned to shout, "It's nothing. Someone looking for the professor."

"Have him come in," the voice ordered.

"But he's looking for the professor, and the professor's not here," the maid replied.

"Have him come in, I tell you."

"Dear Jesus," the maid groaned, as if disaster were imminent. She opened the door and let Laurana in.

Through the succession of open doors a man came walking toward him, an elderly, bent man, with a bright plaid over his shoulders.

"You are looking for my brother?"

"Yes. I'm an old friend of his from the university. He's invited me several times to come see the excavations and the new museum. So today—"

"Please, do come in. He will be home before long." He turned to lead the way and no sooner had he turned than the maid gestured warningly to Laurana; she lifted her right hand to her forehead, in a kind of spiral motion. The unequivocal import of the gesture stopped Laurana. But without having turned around and without turning now, the man said, "Concetta is warning you that I am crazy." Astonished and at the same time heartened by this, Laurana followed him.

At the far end of the perspective, in a study filled with books, statuary, and amphora, the man walked over to a desk, sat down, nodded to Laurana that he should sit down on the other side of the desk. He pushed aside a little barricade of books, and said, "Concetta thinks I'm crazy and, to tell the truth, she's not the only one."

Laurana made a vague gesture of disbelief and protest.

"The trouble is, in some respects I really am. I don't

know whether my brother ever spoke to you about me, if only for the fact that when he was going to the university, I—according to what he says—begrudged him the money for it. . . . I am Benito, the older brother. The name did not come to me from the person you're thinking of, naturally; he and I were of almost the same age. After the unification of Italy, republican revolutionary sentiments were grafted onto my family tree. I am called Benito because an uncle of mine, who died the year I was born, had himself been born the year Benito Juárez had Maximilian shot. The execution of a king was apparently a source of irrepressible joy for my grandfather. This did not prevent him, however, from continuing a tradition of Bonapartist names that had also been established in the family. From the revolution of 1820 on, not one child in our family has escaped having Napoleon as a second or third name, if it was a boy, or Letizia, if it was a girl. As a matter of fact, my brother is called Jerome Napoleon, my sister is Letizia, and behind my Benito Juárez I hide a Joseph Napoleon. But it may well be that there is some ambivalence in the Joseph, as between Mazzini and Bonaparte. It's a good idea, as the saying goes, to travel with a change of clothes. During Fascism, my name used to make a certain impression. Someone who was called Benito and who was the same age as the man directing the great destinies of the fatherland, as we used to put it. . . . People were so accustomed to the Mussolini myth that maybe they got the idea we had started to march on Rome together the instant we'd sprouted our first tooth. . . . You are a Fascist?"

"No, no, quite the contrary."

"Don't be offended. We all are, a little."

"Is that so?" Laurana was both amused and annoyed.

"Of course. I'll give you an example here and now, which happens also to be an instance of one of my recent and keenest disappointments. Peppino Testaquadra is an old friend of mine, a man who from '27 to '43 spent the best years of his life either in prison or under house arrest. If you were to pin the Fascist tag on him, he would jump at your throat or laugh in your face. . . . Yet he is a Fascist."

"A Fascist! You say Testaquadra is a Fascist?"

"You know him?"

"I've heard him speak several times. I read his articles."

"And naturally, judging from his past and from what he says and writes, you maintain that labeling him a Fascist calls for a heavy dose of bad faith—or insanity. Well, insanity perhaps—yes, if we hold insanity to be a kind of free port for truth. But bad faith, absolutely not. He's a friend of mine, I tell you, an old friend. Yet there's nothing for it; a Fascist he is. Someone who contrives to find himself a small niche—perhaps even an uncomfortable niche—in the power structure, and from that niche what does he do? He begins to draw distinctions between the interests of the State and of the individual, the rights of his elector and of his opponent, between convenience and justice. Now, don't you think one could ask Testaquadra who made him suffer prison or house arrest? Doesn't it seem to you we may— maliciously—suppose that he got off on the wrong foot, or that if Mussolini had called on him—"

"Maliciously," Laurana emphasized.

"My malice gives you the measure of the disappointment

and pain Peppino has caused me as a person who voted for
him and as a friend as well."

"You vote for Testaquadra's Party?"

"Not for the Party. That is to say, for the Party, naturally,
but in a secondary sense. Like everyone else . . . One
person is bound to a politician by a favor, a plate of spa-
ghetti, a gun license, a passport. Another person is bound,
like me, by personal esteem, respect, friendship. . . . And
just think what a sacrifice it is for me to leave the house to
go vote for him!"

"You never leave the house?"

"Never, haven't for some years. At one point in my life, I
made a few quite precise calculations: if I leave the house in
search of the company of one intelligent person, one honest
person, I run the risk of meeting en route a dozen thieves
and half as many idiots who stand poised to communicate
to me their views on mankind, the national government, the
city administration, Moravia. . . . Does it seem to you worth
the trouble?"

"No, actually not."

"And then I am very comfortable at home, especially
here." He pointed to the books and gestured as if to gather
them all to him.

"A fine library," Laurana said.

"Not that I can always avoid stumbling into thieves and
idiots even here. I'm speaking of writers, obviously, not
their characters. But I easily get rid of them. I return them
to the bookshop or I present them as a gift to the first fool
who comes to call on me."

"So even by staying at home you don't manage to avoid
fools entirely."

"I do not. But here it's different. I feel more secure, more removed. It's a bit like being at the theater; I even enjoy myself. I can tell you this also: from here, everything that happens in town seems to me pure theater—all the marriages, funerals, quarrels, arrivals, departures. . . . Because I know everything, hear everything, and everything reaches me multiplied, as it were, by echoes—"

"I met someone from Montalmo," Laurana interrupted, "whose name escapes me for the moment. He's tall, with a broad, dark face, wears American-style glasses, and he's a kind of precinct worker for Deputy Abello—"

"You are a teacher?"

"A teacher, yes," Laurana replied. Before the other man's sudden, chill suspicion, he flushed, as if he were concealing a different identity.

"And where did you meet this—this man from Montalmo whose name escapes you?"

"On the steps of the Palazzo di Giustizia a few days ago."

"Was he—how shall I say—enjoying a police escort?"

"Why, no, he was with Deputy Abello and an acquaintance of mine, a lawyer."

"And you want to know from me what his name is?"

"It's not that I'm so anxious to know—"

"But do you or do you not want to know it?"

"Yes."

"Why?"

"Oh, like that, out of curiosity. . . . The man rather impressed me, that's all."

"With reason," Don Benito said, and he burst out laughing.

He laughed until he gasped for breath, until he wept.

Then he grew quiet, and wiped his eyes with a big red handkerchief. He is crazy, Laurana thought. Really and truly crazy.

"Do you know what I'm laughing at?" Don Benito asked. "I'm laughing at myself, at my own fear. . . . I was afraid, I admit it. I consider myself a free man—in a town which is not—but for one moment there I felt that old fear of finding myself caught between the criminal and the cop. But even if you really are from the police—"

"I'm not. I told you, I'm a professor, a colleague of your brother's."

"And who or what makes this professor run head on into Raganà?" He laughed again, then explained: "That question is dictated by caution, not by fear. Anyhow, I've already given you your answer."

"His name is Raganà and he is a criminal."

"Precisely. One of the respectable, unpunished, untouchable criminals."

"Untouchable even today, you think?"

"I don't know. Probably they'll get to him, too. But the fact of the matter is, my dear friend, Italy is a country so blessed that for every weed they destroy, two spring up in its place. I saw something quite like this forty years ago. And it is true in both *la grande* and *la petite histoire* that whereas the first time a phenomenon occurs it is tragic, but the second time round it becomes farcical. In both instances, however, I'm uneasy."

"But what has *then* got to do with *now?*" Laurana exclaimed. "Forty years ago . . . All right, I can even grant that you're right. A big mafia tried to smash the little mafia.

But today—oh, come. Does it look to you like the same thing today?"

"Not the same thing. However, listen to me a moment. I want to tell you something you surely know about already, but the story has a moral. . . . A big industry decides to build a dam above a populated area. Ten or more deputies, acting on the opinion of technical experts, ask that the dam not be built because of the threat it poses to the area below. The government permits the dam to be built. Later, when it has been built and is already in operation, there is some warning of danger. Nothing is done. Nothing until the disaster, which some people had foreseen, actually happens. The result: two thousand people dead. . . . Two thousand—as many people as all the Raganàs who flourish around here liquidate in ten years. And I could tell you a number of other fables but you know them perfectly well."

"The analogy doesn't hold. And, frankly, it seems to me that your story's moral smacks of an apology. You take no account of the fear, the terror—"

"You think the people around Longarone weren't afraid when they looked up at that dam?"

"But that isn't the same. I agree, yes, it was a very serious thing—"

"That will go unpunished exactly as do our choice and more characteristic crimes."

"But, after all, if this Raganà, and all the Raganàs whom we know and don't know—if it is possible finally to get at them in spite of the protection they enjoy, it seems to me that will be a big, a significant step forward."

"You really think so? Given the situation we're in?"

"What situation?"

"A half-million emigrants, which is to say, almost the entire able-bodied population; an agriculture that is completely abandoned; sulphur mines that are closed; salt mines that are about to close; a petroleum industry that is a joke; regional authorities each more addlepated than the next; a national government that lets us stew in our own juice. . . . We are drowning, my friend, drowning. . . . This corsair that has been Sicily, with the splendid leopard rampant on its prow, the Guttuso colors in its great shield, with its crew of headline-seeking *mafiosi* and the politicians secretly in cahoots with them, with its *engagé* writers, its screwed-up logicians, its madmen, its high-noon and nocturnal demons, its oranges and its sulphur and its booted corpses—the ship is sinking, my friend, sinking. And you and I—I mad maybe, and you perhaps *engagé*—with the water already to our knees, we sit here worrying about Raganà, whether he's jumped into the Deputy's lifeboat or stayed aboard with those who are about to die."

"I don't agree," Laurana said.

"All in all, neither do I," Don Benito said.

13   "What animal keeps its pecker in the
ground?" Arturo Pecorilla asked from the
doorway.

Almost nightly, young Pecorilla made his entrance into
the club with a harvest of jokes, puns, and double-entendres
that he diligently garnered from magazines and newspapers
and the variety shows he frequented in the county seat.
When his father was on hand, however, his entrance was
rather subdued and melancholy, as befitted a person suffering from nervous exhaustion, which the young man claimed
to be, to justify his university defections. Notary Pecorilla
conceded that a young man in such a state needed, yes, he
needed lively companionship but he did not have to be the

life of the party. This opinion, although not shared by the doctors, was firmly maintained by the notary and, practical considerations having to be taken into account, was perforce respected by the young man.

That evening, the notary was not at the club, and therefore the young man launched his humorous conundrum about what animal keeps its pecker underground.

Those most familiar with the animal world—the hunters, that is—proposed the woodcock and the anteater; the least informed lapsed into the exotic, suggesting the crane, the stork, ostrich, and condor.

Young Pecorilla let them simmer a bit, then triumphantly announced, "A widow!"

The ensuing chuckles were followed by three reactions in succession. Colonel Salvaggio leaped up from his armchair and, in a voice that promised an imminent explosion of anger, demanded: "Do you include the war widow?"

"Most emphatically not," the young man replied. The Colonel sank back into his chair.

"Your question contains a linguistic lapse," Piranio, the accountant, observed. "You used the word 'keep' rather than 'has.' A Hispanicism, a Neapolitanism."

"Guilty as charged," Arturo Pecorilla said. He did not want to get into any argument; he was eager to tell a brand-new joke.

The reaction of Don Luigi Corvaia was entirely irrelevant, perhaps unthinking, certainly incautious. "Who knows," he said reflectively, "whether the widow of Dr. Roscio will remarry."

"Because she's got her pecker underground?" young Pecorilla said, with the lack of delicacy for which he was renowned.

"You're always putting your foot in it!" Don Luigi shouted, red in the face. The realization that he had made a misstep fueled his rage. And that good-for-nothing young Pecorilla had to go and crudely underline the slip, so that no one could overlook it. Some things were delicate, dangerous even, but all he ever wanted was to turn them into a joke. "I said what I said," Don Luigi explained, forcing himself to be calm, "automatically. I heard the word 'widow' and the thought simply occurred to me—but you have no respect for the living or the dead."

"I was joking," the young man said. "Everyone understood that I was only joking, didn't they? I would never have allowed myself—"

"There are some things one does not joke about. If here, among friends, I wonder out loud what the widow of our poor friend Roscio will do, you can be sure that my intentions are entirely respectful. For that matter, everyone here knows the many good qualities of the Signora"—a chorus of "Naturally" and "Of course," after which Don Luigi continued—"but the Signora is so young and, yes, let's say it frankly, so beautiful, that a man feels a kind of, I don't know, it hurts a man to think that she must remain closed in forever with her grief and her mourning—"

"Indeed, yes," Colonel Salvaggio sighed. "A fine piece of woman."

"But you, sir, at this stage . . ." Arturo Pecorilla observed.

Regretting that he had let the question of war widows drop, he intended now to make the Colonel explode on the subject of manly potency.

"At this stage—I what?" The Colonel gathered himself together in his chair like a panther preparing to leap.

"At this stage . . ." the young man repeated, with a gesture and in a tone of commiseration.

The Colonel leaped. "At my age, with all my seventy-two years, if routinely I do not at least once a day—"

"Colonel, Colonel, I scarcely recognize you," Piranio, the accountant, intervened severely. "Think of your prestige, your rank!"

Because Piranio was sincerely persuaded that a high degree of decorum and solemn self-possession befitted a colonel, his admonishments had an immediate and profound effect.

"You are right," the Colonel said. "You are right. But when I hear myself so basely provoked—"

"Ignore it," Piranio interrupted. It was a scene that was repeated daily, and anyone who wanted to enjoy the Colonel's rages to the full had to take advantage of Piranio's absences.

With the Colonel restored to his armchair, it was Piranio who took up the subject of the widow Roscio. "Young— and beautiful, I agree. But one must remember that she has a little daughter, and perhaps she will want to dedicate herself entirely to the child—"

"Dedicate herself entirely to the child—what does that mean?" the postmaster interrupted. "When there's money, my esteemed friend, no such problem exists. With what her father's left her, the girl's already well off. Put her in a good school, and the problem of her mother's dedication is solved."

"That's right," Don Luigi approved.

"However," Piranio said, "you must consider the other side of the question. A widow with a young daughter, even if financially well off . . . Well, a man thinks twice about marrying her."

"Really! Is there a man present—aside from yourself, of course—who would think twice? About a woman like that? Who wouldn't go after her without a second thought, hook, line, and sinker?" Commendatore Zerillo said.

"Mother of God," the Colonel groaned.

From that moment, respect for the lady went into a dizzying decline. Respect for her body, that is, not for her virtues. Her virtues prejudged rare and untouchable, it was her naked body, and certain parts of her body, that they surveyed and enlarged in perspectives like those the photographer Brandt obsessively captures. The lack of respect reached such proportions that the Colonel attached himself to her breast like a suckling child and it required all Piranio's authority and appeals to the glories of past history to make him let go.

Laurana did not say a word. The vast deal of talk about women that ordinarily went on at the club he followed almost always with amusement. An evening at the club was for him like reading a book—Pirandello or Brancati, depending on the theme and tone of the conversation, but most often, as it happened, the warmly ribald Brancati. That is why he went to the club assiduously; it was the brief respite in his day.

The discussion of Signora Roscio, however, upset and disturbed him, and aroused conflicting responses. He was both outraged and fascinated. More than once he was on the point of leaving or of voicing his indignation, but prurience, malice—even more, a dim pain, something akin to jealousy —drew and held him.

The erotic interlude having subsided, they reverted to the subject of what Commendatore Zerillo dubbed the eligibles: those who, being bachelors between thirty and forty years of age, holding a university degree, possessed of a fine appearance and good character, and with the promise of future success, could aspire to the bed and fortune of the widow Roscio. At a certain point, whether by way of compliment or out of conviction, someone advanced the name of Laurana, and Laurana, flushing, protested as if it were a compliment.

The question was resolved by Don Luigi Corvaia. "What are you looking for?" he said. "When the lady decides to remarry, she's got a husband ready and waiting right in the family."

"And who is that?" the Colonel demanded so threateningly that it seemed he had already snatched up the thunderbolt to hurl at the head of the bridegroom-elect.

"And who could it be? Her cousin, our good friend Rosello." Don Luigi never forgot, when being his most malicious, to bestow a generous expression of friendship on his victim.

"That church mouse?" the Colonel said, and with the marksman's customary precision, his scorn hit the white enamel spittoon at a distance of nine feet.

"Precisely," Don Luigi smiled, preening himself in the mirror of his own perspicacity. "Precisely."

It was a thought that had been troubling Laurana for several days. He had come to it as furnishing the one possible motive for the crime, whereas Don Luigi had come to it out of a taste for gossip and slander. The one thing lacking in the picture—or, rather, the one indecipherable, obscure, contradictory datum that did not fit it was the fact that Roscio should have tried secretly, through the Communist deputy, to strike at Rosello. There were two possibilities: either the wife and cousin had been caught by Roscio in flagrante delicto, as the courts have it; or Roscio merely, although with reason, suspected the infidelity. In the first instance, one would have to ascribe to him a most strange behavior; a man sees the thing with his own eyes, coldly informs his wife's lover that he intends to ruin him, and then turns his back, as it were, and, while he sets about preparing his revenge, maintains an unaltered relationship with the man he hates. In the second instance, one would have to explain how Rosello came to know that Roscio suspected and was plotting to harm him. And there was, yes, there was a third hypothesis: the wife was innocent but had been pursued and tempted by her cousin, and she had alerted her husband or he had realized it himself. In that case, however, Roscio would have been confident of his wife's fidelity and he would have confined himself to changing or breaking off his relationship with the other man.

Given his understanding and tolerance of human passions, had he been confronted by not an irreparable but merely an attempted offense, he would not have been pushed to the point of seeking an irreparable revenge.

Also, one had to consider the fact that he had approached the deputy only to ascertain his availability for an exposé; the doctor had not yet decided, indeed had clearly said that he had still to decide whether to tell the deputy everything or nothing, depending. . . . Depending on what? On whether Rosello, faced with the threat, would have changed his behavior? And in threatening him openly would the doctor have stipulated any condition? So one could only revert to the first hypothesis: to a rather strange kind of behavior, very Continental café-society in style, on the part of a husband who had been deceived but, because he was in love with his wife, was tenaciously resolved to keep her. And although Laurana was a severe judge of a life governed by the passions, and most particularly the passions of self-love and honor, he could not help noticing in his hypothesis a lack of respect for Roscio's memory; accordingly, he strove to demolish, dissolve it. But however he revolved the affair, turning it this way and that, it possessed some equivocal, ambiguous element, even though the relationships of cause and effect were still unclear, as were those of the protagonists among themselves and those details in the mechanism of the crime that he knew to be facts. And in that equivocation, that ambiguity, he felt himself morally and sensually involved.

14   Were a trial to be played out on the basis of three clues that were only partly proved and of a motive that was barely discernible through the curtains of gossip, and were that trial to result in a sentence of guilty, Laurana would have found here grounds to bolster his instinctive repugnance for (and his intellectual polemic against) the administration of justice and against the very principle on which the administration of justice was founded. Yet the three clues and the one vague motive that he kept privately debating and juggling now seemed to him to be sufficient, and to leave no margin of doubt about Rosello's guilt.

As the rector of Sant'Anna said, Rosello was, in truth, a

cretin who was not bereft of cunning. With abominable guile, he follows a pattern by no means new in the history of crime to plot his own crime. But he takes no account of the paper from which he snips the words for his death message, because to him the *Osservatore Romano* is a paper like any other, accustomed as he is to seeing it always about the house and in the circles he frequents; and this is his first mistake. Then, his second mistake: he lets enough time pass for Roscio to move, to talk with someone; yet perhaps this was an unavoidable mistake, since one cannot conceive and execute a crime from one day to the next. Third, while the Branca cigar is floating like a balloon in the investigations and news reports, he appears in public in the company of the assassin.

Of course, it is one thing to be privately persuaded that a man is guilty and a very different thing to express that certainty, black on white, in the form of charges or a sentence. But, Laurana thought, perhaps the policeman or the judge found an essential element of his opinion or his judgment in the physical appearance of the suspect or the accused—in his posture, glance, hesitations, starts, speech, all these being things that can be divined from news accounts only with great difficulty. It was this physical element that finally made him feel sure of Rosello's guilt. There are, as everyone knows, cases in which innocent people behave as if they were guilty and are thereby lost; for that matter, under the eye of the local policeman, the customs officer, the carabiniere, or the judge, all Italians begin to act guilty. But he, Laurana, was far from the reaches of the law, far from those invested with the authority of the law—farther

from them than Mars is distant from Earth; he viewed po-
licemen and judges through the lenses of fantasy as Mar-
tians who now and then materialized in human grief, in
madness.

From the day Laurana had asked him about the person
who was accompanying him down the steps of the Palazzo
di Giustizia, Rosello had lost his head. Often he avoided
Laurana, scarcely nodding to him if he could not slip around
a corner or pretend not to see him; but sometimes he but-
tonholed him with protestations of friendship, volunteered
to use his good offices, his influence with government ad-
ministrators, undersecretaries, and Ministers in Laurana's
behalf. Since Laurana was embarrassed by these demonstra-
tions of regard and replied stiffly that he had no need of
being recommended to the powers that be in the educational
bureaucracy, Rosello became suspicious and somber. Perhaps
he thought Laurana did not respond to his show of friendship, did not want to take advantage of the favors he offered,
because of the scorn, rare though it now be, of the honest
man for the criminal; or he may even have thought Laurana
wanted to confide his suspicions to the marshal or the commissioner—in a word, to bring his suspicions, directly or
otherwise, to the attention of the investigators. This intention Laurana absolutely did not have, and his apprehension,
his mortal concern, was precisely that Rosello should at-
tribute any such intention to him. More than the insinuat-
ing fear that was quickened by the memory of how Roscio
and the pharmacist had met their end and that at times
caused him, even automatically, to take precautions that
might spare him the same end, Laurana had a kind of ob-

scure pride which made him decisively reject the idea that just punishment should be administered to the guilty one through any intervention of his. His had been a human, intellectual curiosity that could not, and should not, be confused with the interest of those whom society and State paid to capture and consign to the vengeance of the law persons who transgress or break it. At play in this obscure pride were the centuries of contempt that an oppressed people, an eternally vanquished people, had heaped on the law and all those who were its instruments; a conviction, still unquenched, held that the highest right and truest justice, if one really cares about it, if one is not prepared to entrust its execution to fate or to God, can come only from the barrels of a gun.

At the same time, however, he had an uneasy sense of involuntary complicity, a kind of solidarity, as inappropriate as it was remote, with Rosello and his hired assassin; whatever his moral indignation, his repugnance, this feeling argued conversely for granting them impunity and even for restoring the sense of security that his curiosity had undoubtedly forced them in the last while to forfeit. On the other hand, was it possible to grant Rosello such impunity as would allow him to replace his victim beside the woman who, in Laurana's mind, glowed so obscenely, as if at the inner core of a labyrinth of passion and death? Here even sensuality and desire became ambiguous: unjustified, gratuitous jealousy, charged with all the dissatisfactions, timidities, and repressions of a lifetime, on the one hand; a bitter pleasure, almost the appeasing of desire in a kind of visual panderage, on the other. But all this in a feverish, hallucinatory blur.

And thus passed the whole month of October.

In early November, four days of vacation falling between All Souls' Day and Armistice Day, Laurana discovered that not only do all troubles befall a man from not knowing enough to stay quietly in his own home but that staying at home opened pleasurable vistas of work and reading. The morning of November 2nd, he went out to accompany his mother to the cemetery; after they had ascertained that the graves of their dead did not lack the flowers and lamps they had ordered and paid for, his mother wanted to walk along the cemetery paths, as she did every year, pausing to recite a prayer before the graves of relatives and friends. Accordingly, they stopped in front of the family vault of the Rosellos, where they found the Signora Luisa, in elegant mourning, kneeling in prayer on a velvet cushion before the marble slab that bore the name of her husband "tragically snatched from the bosom of his family." Mounted in the center was an enameled portrait of poor Roscio, who looked twenty years younger but also appeared torn between terror and grief. The Signora rose and did the honors of the house; she explained that she had chosen that youthful likeness of her husband because it was the one nearest to the time when they had first known each other; she detailed the genealogy of all the dead entombed in the walls of the chapel and their degree of closeness, whether by consanguinity or marriage tie, to herself—to her, the living, yes, but how unhappily, accursedly alive. She sighed and brushed away invisible tears. Old Signora Laurana recited her prayer. As they said goodbye, it seemed to Laurana that when Signora Luisa shook his hand, she held it for one meaningful moment and that there was a gleam of imploring understanding in her eyes. He imagined that her cousin, her lover, might have told her everything, and that therefore she was urging him to remain silent. He was deeply disturbed, for that confirmed her direct complicity.

But there was no need to urge silence on him. On the contrary, his decision to spend every evening at home sprang from a wish to forget and to be forgotten, to restore to Rosello the security and freedom he had lacked in the last weeks. And to her, too, to the Signora Luisa, for how frightened she must feel to be driven to such funereal zeal, kneeling for hours before her husband's grave while she waited for some visit to bring her the relief of rising to her feet. That movement, Laurana noted, was attentively awaited and spied upon by a group of young bloods nearby, for even in the immobility of prayer and meditation, the close-fitting black dress allowed a glimpse of the abundant, languid nudity of a Delacroix odalisque, and as the Signora got up she had necessarily to expose a further whiteness of thigh above her tightly drawn stockings. What a people, he thought, but his contempt was shot through with jealousy. Any and every place in the world where the hem of a skirt was rising a fraction of an inch above the knee, there, within a range of thirty yards, was bound to be a Sicilian, one at least, to spy on the phenomenon. Laurana did not stop to think that he, too, had voraciously caught the white gleam

of flesh between black and black, and that he had noticed
the group of young hoodlums for the simple reason that he
was of the same breed.

Leaning on his arm as she walked, his mother whispered
to him her prognostication for the widow Roscio: she would
not be slow to remarry.

"Why?" he asked.

"Why, because life is like that. And then she's so young,
so beautiful."

"What about you, did you remarry?"

"I was not so young any more, and beautiful I have never
been," the old woman said, with a sigh.

Laurana had a disagreeable sensation akin to disgust. It's
strange, he thought. When you walk through a cemetery,
you feel so bestially alive. Maybe it's the weather today.
For the day was particularly beautiful, warm and with a de-
cayed but pleasant smell of earth and roots; the cemetery
was permeated also with the perfume of thickets of wild
mint, rosemary, carnations, and, near the wealthier mauso-
leums, of roses as well.

"And whom should she marry, according to you?" he
asked, with some irritation.

"Why, her cousin the lawyer—Rosello," the old woman
said, pausing to scrutinize his face.

"Why him, of all people?"

"Why, because they grew up together, in the same house.
Because they know each other well. Because their marriage
can reunify a property."

"These seem like good reasons to you? The whole idea

strikes me as obscene, and especially so because they grew up together in the same house."

"You know the old saying: Beware of cousins, brothers-in-law, and godfathers. The most serious missteps almost always happen with relatives and godparents—"

"Was there a misstep?"

"Who knows? Once upon a time, of course, when they were young, when they lived under the same roof, people said they were in love. Puppy love, naturally. . . . But the Dean did not take to the idea, so people said, and he put a stop to it. I don't remember too clearly now but there was some such talk."

"Why did he put a stop to it? If they were in love, he could have let things develop to the point of marriage."

"Just now you said it seems obscene to you. The Dean thought the same then."

"I called it obscene because you didn't mention love. The reason you brought out for an eventual marriage was the fact that they had grown up in the same house, and then the matter of property. But if it was a question of love, that was different."

"Marriage between cousins requires the dispensation of the Church, so some shadow of sin there is. Do you suppose the Dean could admit that any love which was not completely honorable could be born in his house? It would have been a disgrace. The Dean is a most scrupulous man."

"And now?"

"Now what?"

"If they marry now, I mean. Isn't it the same thing? A lot of people will think as you do—that they loved each other from the beginning, from the time they both lived in the Dean's house."

"It isn't the same thing. Now it becomes almost an act of charity. To marry a widow with a child, to reunify property—"

"An act of charity to reconsolidate property?"

"And why not? Property must be treated with charity, too."

Christ, what a religion! Laurana thought. But, for that matter, his mother testified daily to this religion of property, never allowing the stale bread, the leftovers, the fruit that was beginning to turn, to be thrown out. "It hurts me," she would say, and she ate the hard bread and the overripe pears. And because of the loving care she evinced for the meal's leftovers by eating them—almost as if they begged for the grace of becoming feces—there was the risk that one time or another she herself would be carried off.

"Suppose these two did love each other when they lived under the Dean's roof, and went on loving each other even after her marriage? And suppose that, at a certain point, they decided to get Roscio out of the way?"

"That's impossible," the old woman said. "The poor doctor, as everybody knows, died because of the pharmacist."

"But what if the pharmacist died because of Roscio?"

"That's impossible," the old woman said again.

"All right, so it's impossible. But for a moment let us agree that it is possible. Would you call that an act of charity?"

"Worse things have been known to happen," the old

woman said, not in the slightest scandalized. They had just reached the grave of the pharmacist Manno, who, under the wings of an angel, looked out from his enamel medallion, smiling with satisfaction over a lucky hunting trip.

15   Laurana spent the four days of vacation ordering and updating the notes for his
Italian and history classes. He was passionately scrupulous
about his work and so, being busy with these tasks, he almost managed to forget the affair in which he had got himself embroiled; whenever he did think of it, he saw it as de-
tached and distant, in style, form, and also somewhat in
content delineated rather in the manner of a Graham
Greene novel. And yet the meeting with Signora Luisa in
the cemetery and the thoughts that that meeting had
aroused in him had flowed into a literary circuit with ca-
dences of an unregenerate, catholic romanticism.

The morning he resumed the routine of the school week,

now all the more onerous after four days of rest, to his surprise he found the widow Roscio on the bus bound for the county seat.

She was sitting up front, her black-stockinged legs in line with the open door. The seat beside her was free and, replying to his bow with a timidly inviting smile, she gestured toward it. Laurana hesitated. A feeling of shame—almost as if were he seated beside her, in the first row, he would be displaying for everyone to see all that he knew and all the desire and revulsion that he felt—drove him for a moment to seek an excuse to evade the invitation. His eye searched among the seats to the rear for some friend to whom he might have something to say, but the only people sitting in the back were farmers and students, and furthermore all the places were taken. He accepted with thanks. The Signora said how lucky it was for her that the seat had remained free until then, since in this way she would have someone beside her to whom she could talk, for conversation was the one thing that enabled her to overcome the discomfort she felt on buses, although she did not suffer at all in a car or even on a train. She then spoke of the weather, which was beautiful; and of Saint Martin's summer, which was a true, real summer; of the olive harvest, which was good; of her uncle the Dean, who was poorly. . . . She talked with a meandering and mindless volubility that was ear-punishing. Laurana actually felt as if his ears were stopped, as happens when a person descends swiftly from mountaintop to valley. Not that he was descending from any lofty peak; he was emerging from sleep, from the testiness of the alarm clock, and the flatness of the cup of weak coffee his mother had prepared for him. But sensation returned to him also, directly from blood that grew hot as he sat beside her. The more closely, the more pitilessly he observed her to detect some mortal flaw, to uncover some perversity, the more abundant the grace of her body; her face with lips curved in pouting invitation, her heavy hair, her perfume that barely concealed the acrid scent of bed and of sleep, aroused in him a painful, a physically painful, desire.

How curious it was; before Roscio's death, he had met her many times, had often found himself in conversation with her. A beautiful woman, no denying that, but like how many others, especially today when the canons of feminine beauty are, thanks to the assorted myths of the films, so vast and varied as to embrace fragility and opulence, the profile of Arethusa and the jaw of a fishwife. It takes a guest of iron, he thought, to celebrate the banquet. She had seemed to him particularly beautiful, particularly desirable as she sat in her mourning clothes under the enlarged portrait of her husband in that little parlor where, because of her living presence, the presence of her young, rounded, knowing body, the half-drawn curtains, the lighted lamps, and the shrouded mirrors had conferred on Roscio's dead presence a dark, derisive halo. And then, to feed, to complicate his aroused desire had come the revelation of the crime—of the passion, the betrayal, the cold perfidy with which it had been planned; evil had become incarnate, had been obscurely, splendidly transformed into sex. Laurana recognized in his turmoil the remoras of a long-ago indoctrination in sin—the turn of the screw, in a word—and of a terror about sexual things that he had never shaken off; indeed, the more actively his mind was engaged, the more fiercely they assailed him. Therefore he felt—especially now, sitting beside her, with her body lurching against his at each abrupt curve —he felt as if he were divided and dichotomized. And the myth of divisions and dichotomizations that he had always found so provocative in literature was now verified in his own life.

As they left the bus, Laurana did not know what to do, whether to take his leave or to accompany her wherever she had to go. They stood for a moment in the piazza, and then the Signora suddenly abandoned the fatuous manner she had sustained throughout the trip; the lines of her face hardened as she said she had come to the county seat that day for a reason which she wished to confide in him. "I've discovered that my husband actually did go to Rome to see that deputy friend of his," she said. "And he went to ask him what you told me that evening—you remember?— when you came to my house with my cousin." At the word "cousin," her mouth twisted almost in disgust.

"Really?" Caught off guard, Laurana sought rapidly to account for this unforeseeable confidence.

"Yes. I found it out almost by accident, when I'd given up any hope. . . . Because what you told me that evening brought back so many things, so many little things that, once they were pieced together, made it quite possible that what you had learned by accident was—might be true. So I began to look and look, and finally I came across a diary my husband used to keep, unbeknownst to me. He'd hidden it behind a row of books. When I'd given up all hope, even though I did keep on looking like mad, quite by coincidence I happened to take down a book I felt like reading, and there it was."

"A diary. He kept a diary."

"One of those fat appointment books that drug suppliers send doctors. . . . Every day, starting with January 1st, in that almost indecipherable doctor's script of his, he had jotted down three or four lines about whatever he thought should be recorded, especially things that had to do with our daughter. Then, early in April, he began to write about someone whom he didn't name—"

"Whom he didn't name?" Laurana asked, with suspicious irony.

"No, he didn't name the person, but it's clear who it is."

"Oh, it is clear," Laurana said, in a tone that indicated his condescending willingness to carry on the joke without being taken in by it.

"Clear. No possible doubt. It's my cousin."

This Laurana did not expect. He caught his breath, and his jaw sagged.

"I am confiding in you," the Signora continued, "because I know what friendship, what affection, you felt for my husband. This is something that no one knows, that no one must know about until I have the proofs in hand. And today I have come here to find them. I have a suspicion where."

"But then—" Laurana said.

"Then what?"

He was about to say that then she had had no part in it;

she was innocent; he had suspected her unjustly. But, blushing, he said, "Then you no longer believe your husband was killed because he was with the pharmacist?"

"This, in all conscience, I still cannot say, but it is possible. . . . And you?"

"I?"

"Are you convinced?"

"Convinced of what?"

"That my cousin is responsible and that the pharmacist had nothing to do with it."

"Really—"

"Please. Don't hide anything from me. I so need you," the Signora said pitifully, looking into his eyes with luminous supplication.

"I am not really convinced. Let's say I have some suspicions, some rather strong suspicions, for that matter. But you—would you be willing to take action against your cousin?"

"And why not? If the death of my husband . . . But I need your help."

"I am at your service," Laurana stammered.

"First, you must promise me you will say nothing, not even to your mother, about what I have told you."

"I swear to you I will not."

"Then, from what you know and from what I hope to find out today, we can talk it over together, discuss it together, and decide on some course of action."

"But one must be cautious, prudent. . . . It's one thing to be suspicious—"

"Today I hope to make sure."

"How?"

"That's nothing to talk about here and anyway it would be premature. I will stay in the city until tomorrow evening, and tomorrow evening, if you are willing, we could meet. . . . Where could we meet?"

"Well, I don't know. . . . I mean, I don't know whether you would mind being seen in public with me—"

"I wouldn't mind."

"In a café."

"In a café, very well."

"The Café Romeris, then. There are never very many people, and one can have some privacy."

"Around seven? At seven?"

"Isn't that a little late for you?"

"Not at all. Furthermore, I don't believe I will have done all I must do before seven. Between today and tomorrow I have a difficult job to do. But tomorrow you will know everything. . . . At seven, then, at the Café Romeris. We can catch the last train and go back home together, if you don't mind."

"No, I will be delighted," Laurana said, flushing with happiness.

"And your mother, what will you tell your mother?"

"I'll say that I must stay late on school business. It won't be the first time, for that matter."

"You promise?" the Signora said, and her smile was full of promise.

"On my word." Laurana was swept up on a wave of joy.

"Until tomorrow, then," the Signora said, and held out her hand.

In a flood of love and remorse, Laurana bowed over her hand, almost as if he were about to kiss it. He stood looking after her for a moment as she walked across the piazza, filled with the green of palms and the blue of the sky—a marvelous, innocent, courageous creature. He was near to tears.

16 The Café Romeris's décor was Art Nouveau; its tall mirrors were embellished by decalcomania lions advertising the restorative Bisleri Tonic; the *baiser au serpent* carved on the front of the counter seemed to prolong its tentacles in the feet of tables and chairs, in the branching lamps, even in the cup handles. The café now lived more in the pages of a writer of that city, dead these thirty years, than in the patronage of the townspeople. The scarce clientele comprised foreigners, people from the province who recalled its past splendor, or people like Laurana, who preferred it for its quiet and its literary associations. It was by no means clear why Signor Romeris, last in a glorious dynasty of confectioners, still kept it open; perhaps he, too, for literary reasons, in honor of the writer who had frequented and immortalized it.

Laurana arrived at ten to seven. He had rarely been at the Romeris at that hour, but the same people were there as in the morning or early afternoon: Signor Romeris behind the cash register; Baron d'Alcozer, half asleep; His Excellency Mosca and His Excellency Lumia, retired judges who, having attained the highest position on the bench, had for some years now been relishing each his pension, game of checkers, glass of Marsala, and cigar.

Laurana knew them. He bowed and was greeted by them all, even by the Baron, who was the least prompt to recognize people. His Excellency Mosca inquired whatever brought him there at that unaccustomed hour. Laurana explained that he had missed the bus and had to wait for the last train. He sat down at a corner table and requested Signor Romeris to fetch him a cognac. Signor Romeris rose heavily to his feet from behind the brass monument to Liberty Style that was his cash register, for he could not permit himself the luxury of a waiter; he poured the cognac with ritual slowness and brought it to Laurana's table. Since Laurana had already taken a book from his pocket, Signor Romeris asked what book it might be. "Voltaire's love letters," Laurana said.

"Aha, aha," chuckled the Baron. "Voltaire's love letters."

"Do you know them?" Laurana asked.

"My friend," the Baron said, "I know all of Voltaire."

"But who reads him any more today?" Judge Lumia said.

"I do," Judge Mosca said.

"Well, we read him, yes. And so does the professor here,

I don't know to what extent. But with the world going as it does, you wouldn't say that Voltaire is a widely read author today, or at least not that he's rightly understood," Judge Lumia said.

"Ah, that no." The Baron sighed.

Laurana let the subject drop. For that matter, at the Café Romeris, the conversation among the old gentlemen was like this: long pauses while everyone ruminated privately over the matter at hand, with now and then a few remarks exchanged. Fifteen minutes later, indeed, His Excellency Mosca said, "Those dogs don't read Voltaire any more." In the lexicon of the Café Romeris, "dog" was synonymous with "politician."

"Voltaire? They don't read anything, not even the papers," the Baron said.

"There are Marxists who haven't read a single page of Marx," Signor Romeris said.

"And Populists"—the Baron persisted in calling Christian Democrats by the Party's old name—"Populists who haven't read one page of Don Sturzo."

"Ugh, Don Sturzo," Judge Mosca said, grunting his satiety.

Silence fell once more. It was already seven-fifteen. Without retaining the sense of what he read, Laurana was scanning a letter of Voltaire's, doubly obscene in the Italian version, and glancing continually up at the door. Yet everyone knows that a tardiness of fifteen minutes to a half hour is part of a woman's normal concept of time; so he was not impatient, only restless with a restlessness in which he had tossed for the last two days. A joyous restlessness matched by an apprehension in which Luisa (as he now called her to himself) and he, side by side, were stepping into a situation not unlike the Last Judgment: a confrontation with the elderly Signora Laurana.

At quarter to eight, Baron d'Alcozer said to Signor Romeris, with patently provocatory intent: "For that matter, not even your Don Luigi read him," alluding to the writer who had conferred immortality on the Café Romeris and to whose memory Signor Romeris dedicated a jealous, altogether fanatical devotion.

Signor Romeris's head and shoulders straightened behind his cash register. "What has Don Luigi got to do with it?" he said. "Don Luigi read everything, he knew everything. But Voltaire had no place in his world view anyhow. It's a completely different matter."

"But, dear Commendatore Romeris," Judge Mosca said, "I grant you, yes, Don Luigi's view of the world had nothing in common with Voltaire's, but that telegram to Mussolini, and the beret and tassel that he wore on occasion—"

"Excellency, excuse me, but did you by any chance not take the Fascist loyalty oath?" Signor Romeris said, blood in his eye, scarcely containing himself.

"I did not," Judge Lumia said, raising a hand.

"That I wouldn't know," Judge Mosca said.

"Oh, you wouldn't?" Judge Lumia was offended.

"Well, yes, I do," His Excellency admitted, "but it was an accident. They overlooked giving you the oath."

"It was no accident. I saw to it that I escaped taking the oath."

"All the same," Judge Mosca said, "the oath was a necessity of life for us. Either you eat what's set in front of you or out the window you go."

"Whereas Don Luigi—" The Baron snickered.

"In this town," Signor Romeris said, "people's hearts are corroded by envy. Don Luigi Pirandello has written books that the whole world admires, but here he's just the man who once sent a telegram to Mussolini and sometimes wore the Fascist cap. . . . Fools' talk, lunatics' talk . . ." But no one picked up the inference, the insult, for the three old men were content to have irritated their friend.

In other circumstances, Laurana would have been vastly amused; now the little exchange made him impatient, almost as if that were the reason Luisa was late. He stood up, went to the door, opened it, looked right and left along the street. Nothing. He went back and sat down.

"Are you waiting for someone?" Signor Romeris asked.

"No," he said shortly. To himself he said, "She won't come now. It's already eight o'clock." But still he hoped.

He ordered, to the astonishment of Signor Romeris, a second cognac.

At quarter past eight, His Excellency Mosca asked him, "And school, Professor, how's school going?"

"Badly," Laurana replied.

"And why should it go well?" the Baron asked. "If everything's going to the dogs, the school's got to go to the dogs, too."

"That's right," Judge Lumia said.

At quarter to nine, a vision of Luisa dead infiltrated Laurana's apprehensive imagination. He was tempted to tell the four old men what was happening to him, what he felt; certainly they had more experience in the facts of life and the human heart than he. But Baron d'Alcozer, pointing to the book Laurana had closed, began to explain that Voltaire had written these love letters to his own niece and because they were, to say the least, most explicit, he asked Laurana for the book in order to read some passages to his friends.

They were hugely diverted, to Laurana's disgust. How could anyone talk about his anxiety or pain to old men so far gone in malice and obscenity? All in all, better to go to the police, find a responsible, understanding officer, and tell him. . . . Tell him what? That a woman had asked him to meet her at the Café Romeris and then had not come? Ridiculous. Explain the reasons for his apprehension? That would set dangerous, irreversible machinery in motion. And furthermore what did he know of what Luisa had managed to learn in the last two days? Suppose she had found proofs that led in some other direction? Or had not found even a glimmer of proof? Or if the child had fallen sick, or for some other unforeseeable reason she'd been unexpectedly called home? Or if, in the fever of her search, she had forgotten the appointment?

But behind all these probabilities shimmered the vision of her in danger, of her dead.

He strode furiously between door and bar.

"Is something worrying you?" the Baron interrupted his reading to ask.

"No, it's just that I've been here for two hours."

"We've been here for years," the Baron said, closing the book and handing it back to him.

Laurana slipped it inside his briefcase. He looked at his

watch: nine-twenty. "I'd better start out for the station," he said.

"You've got three-quarters of an hour before your train leaves," Signor Romeris said.

"I'll take a little walk; it's a beautiful evening," Laurana said. He paid for the two cognacs, said good night, and left. As he was closing the door behind him, he heard His Excellency Lumia say, "He's got an appointment with a woman, and can't wait."

There were few people on the street. The evening was beautiful, but windy and chill. He walked slowly down toward the station, mulling over dark thoughts in his head.

As he turned into the station square, a car went by him, came to a squealing stop thirty feet ahead, then backed up. The window rolled down and the driver, leaning across the seat, called, "Professor! Professor Laurana!" Laurana went over and recognized someone from town, although for the moment he could not remember the man's name.

"Are you going to the station? For the train back to town?"

"Yes," Laurana said.

"If you'd like a lift . . ." the man offered.

Here's a bit of luck, Laurana thought. He'd get home quickly and would even be able to phone Luisa's home for some word. "Thanks," he said. He got in beside the driver. The car roared off.

17   "A closed sort, a man of few words, impatient at times, irritable. One of those people who are agreeable, yes, and anxious to please, perhaps even warmhearted, but who are capable of reacting unpredictably, who can fly into a rage over a wrong impression or a misunderstood word. I'd have only the best to say of him as a teacher: most competent, meticulous, conscientious. A solid background, sound teaching methods. . . . On that score, let me repeat, there's nothing to be said against him. But as far as his private life is concerned . . . Well, I wouldn't like to be indiscreet, but insofar as private feelings are concerned, as a man he has always seemed to me, how shall I say, full of complexes, obsessed—"

132

"Obsessed?"

"Maybe the word's a little strong, and certainly it doesn't at all fit the impression most people have of him or of his life. They think of him as having an even-tempered, balanced disposition, as being very regular in his habits, frank in expressing his opinions and judgments, liberal. . . . But, now and then, anyone who knows him well has seen him turn thorny, bitter. . . . With women—with the teachers and students here—he seems like a misogynist. But I think he's simply timid."

"Obsessed as far as women go, then, obsessed about sex, that is," the Commissioner said.

"Something like that," the principal agreed.

"And yesterday? How did he behave yesterday?"

"Normally, I'd say. He met all his classes, he talked a little with me, and with other teachers. . . . It seems to me that we talked about Borgese."

The Commissioner's pencil was jotting notes in his little book. "Why?" he asked.

"Why were we talking about Borgese? Only because, for some time now, Laurana has had it in his head that Borgese's been underestimated and that he should be given his just due."

"And you are not of that opinion?" the Commissioner asked, with a hint of suspicion.

"In all conscience, I wouldn't know. I'd have to reread him. . . . His *Rubè* made a tremendous impression on me, but that was thirty years ago, my dear Commissioner, thirty years ago."

"Oh," the Commissioner said, and with nervous jabs of his pencil he crossed out the Borgese clue.

"But perhaps," the principal went on, "it was the day before yesterday that we spoke of Borgese. Yesterday . . . It doesn't seem to me there was anything different, anything changed about him yesterday."

"It is a fact, however, that yesterday he did not stay in the city for a meeting here at the school."

"Definitely not."

"Why did he tell his mother such a thing?"

"Who knows? He wanted to hide something from her, obviously. And the only thing one can think of that he would want to hide from her is some relationship with a woman, or if not exactly a relationship—"

"A meeting, an appointment. We've thought of that. But, up to this point, we've not been able to reconstruct how he spent his time after he left the restaurant near here—that is, from two-thirty on."

"A boy in his class," the principal said, "told me this morning that last evening he saw him at the Café Romeris, sitting at a table."

"Could I speak with this boy?"

The principal had him called at once. The boy confirmed that the evening before, as he was passing the Café Romeris, he had glanced in and had seen Professor Laurana seated at a table; he was reading a book; it was around seven-forty-five, perhaps eight o'clock.

The boy was dismissed. The Commissioner put notebook and pencil back in his pocket and, with a sigh, stood up. "We'll go over to the Café Romeris. I've got to get this business settled quickly. His mother's been at headquarters since six this morning, waiting."

"Poor old woman—he was so attached to his mother," the principal said.

"Who knows?" the Commissioner said. An idea occurred to him and presently he had it confirmed at the Café Romeris.

"According to me," Judge Lumia said, "he had an appointment with a woman. He was impatient, nervous."

"He was waiting for the time to pass. He was wrought up, like a boy on the brink of his first adventure," the Baron said.

"You're mistaken, my dear Baron," Romeris said. "According to me, he had the appointment here and the woman didn't come."

"I don't know," Judge Mosca said, "I don't know. A woman's mixed up in it, no question about that. When he went out, after waiting two hours, one of us said he was running off to an appointment with some woman—"

"I said that," Judge Lumia said.

"But his behavior—really, it wasn't the behavior of someone who has to kill a little time before an appointment. He kept glancing up from his book to look toward the door, he walked back and forth between the door and the bar, and once, as a matter of fact, he opened the door to look up and down the street in both directions," Judge Mosca said.

"So," the Commissioner said, "he didn't know which way the woman would be coming from, whether from the left or right. Which allows one to deduce that he didn't know which part of the city she lived in."

"Let's not deduce anything," the Baron said. "Reality is always richer, more unpredictable than our deductions. But if you do want to deduce something, I will tell you this— that if he was really waiting for a woman, here in this café, then it must have been a woman from out of town. . . . What do you think, that women here leave the house at seven or eight at night to go to an appointment in some café?"

"Unless it was a whore," His Excellency Lumia corrected him.

"He wasn't a man to have anything to do with whores," Signor Romeris said.

"Dear Commendatore Romeris, you have no idea how many people—serious, decently behaved, cultivated people —go looking for the company of whores," Judge Lumia said. "What's more likely is that a whore would have given him an appointment at her house or in a hotel. Here, if anything, one would expect a lovers' meeting."

"The problem is this," the Baron said. "He had an appointment here, he waits two hours, the woman doesn't come, he leaves the café saying that he is going to the station, and he disappears. Or he stays here until it's time for the appointment, goes to keep it, and disappears. Let's suppose he was waiting for the woman here. When he realizes that he's been stood up or that the woman hasn't been able to come for who knows what reason—humiliated or worried, as the case may be—what can he do? There are three possibilities: he goes home to sweat out his disappointment or his concern in his own bed; or he goes to the woman's house to demand an explanation, and finds someone who finishes him off; or he goes and throws himself off a cliff or under a train. He did not go home, so the other two possibilities remain open. If he was here just to kill time and then went to an appointment, one of the two possibilities remains open: that at the place of the appointment he finds a husband or a father or a brother who does him in and good night."

"But another hypothesis is possible, after all, one which is less romantic but more likely, more natural. He went to the appointment, found the woman of his desire, and with her forgot his mother and the school and the good Lord, too. Isn't that possible?" Judge Mosca said.

"I don't believe so," Signor Romeris said. "Such a quiet, controlled man—"

"Exactly," Judge Lumia said.

The Commissioner stood up. "My head's in a whirl," he said. The Baron's line of reasoning, unquestionably sound and precise, had opened an abyss before him. He would go find them all, all the women who could have had a brief or long-standing relationship with the professor. To start with: all the students at school—girls between fifteen and eighteen today are capable of anything. Then the women teachers. Then the mothers of students, both boys and girls, or at least the better-preserved, attractive ones. And then the easy women, the whores who could be called honest, as in the old days, and the others, the newer kind that worked by the hour. A job without end. . . . Unless, of course, the professor were to turn up at home between today and tomorrow, like a cat that had gone out to spend a few nights on the rooftops.

But the professor was lying under a heavy pile of lime, in an abandoned sulphur mine halfway, as the crow flies, between his home town and the county seat.

18   September 8th. In town, the Feast of
Mary the Child: the effigy of an infant
swathed in gold cloth and pearls and carried in procession;
fireworks and band music, to which the very walls vibrated
like the diapason; the first hog-butchering and the final
inundation of water ices of the season; and Dean Rosello's
resumption of his habit of receiving friends at home, in
homage to Mary the Child, whose altar in the mother
church he particularly fancied. The custom was years old,
but the year before he had omitted the reception because
it behooved him to observe a period of mourning on the
occasion of Roscio's death. Now, the first anniversary of
that death having occurred in August, he reopened his house

139

for the feast day, with the further reason that the betrothal of his nephew the lawyer and his niece Luisa was to be announced, an event, the Dean said, in which had conspired the ill will of men and the inscrutable will of God, to the second of which he submitted.

"I am resigned to it, quite simply," he explained to Don Luigi Corvaia. "The Lord knows, I would not have wished a marriage between these two, growing up as they did in my own house like brother and sister, but at this point, after the tragedy, it is a matter of charity. Charity within the family, naturally. Could my poor niece—young as she is—be left with a child, to spend the rest of her life alone? And on the other hand, given the times we live in, how to find her a good husband, a man who would not marry her to gobble up all she's got, and one who would have the goodness of heart, the charity, to consider the child as his own? Very difficult, dear Don Luigino, very difficult. . . . So my nephew, who, to tell the truth, is not at all the marrying sort of man, decided—I won't say to sacrifice himself, for Heaven's sake, but to take this step out of a sense of justice and compassion."

"Christ!" This, like a bellow, from Colonel Salvaggio, who, standing behind the Dean, had overheard the last remark.

With equal parts of indignation and alarm, the Dean turned around, but, seeing the Colonel, permitted himself to smile, and admonished him gently. "Colonel, Colonel, always the same. . . ."

"Forgive me," the Colonel said. "What I meant was that because of the cloth you wear, you rightly call it compassion, but I, old sinner that I am, would call it by another name.

In all events, Signora Luisa is a splendid woman, and your nephew, good God, is a man. Now, I say that a man who is a man, when he is confronted by beauty, by loveliness—"

Threatening him with a playful hand, the Dean moved away, and the Colonel continued in a freer vein with Don Luigi. "He talks to me about compassion, that nasty little priest. A woman—God knows what I'd not do to be with a woman like that—" he gestured toward her as she stood, very elegant in her mourning, by the side of her cousin fiancé. She noticed him and replied with a smile and a slight nod of her head. The Colonel shivered and leaned down to groan his desire into Don Luigi's ear. "You see that smile? When she smiles, it's as if she were stepping right out of her clothes. And what that does to me—" Abruptly raising his arm as if he were grasping a saber, he shouted, "Charge, for the love of God, charge!" Seeing him lunge forward, Don Luigi thought he was about to hurl himself on the lady, but the Colonel was hurrying toward the buffet where they had begun to hand out ices.

Don Luigi moved toward the buffet also. There were the rector of Sant'Anna, the notary Pecorilla with his wife, the Signora Zerillo. In half sentences and under their breath, they were speaking ill of the other guests. Naturally. But Don Luigi was not in the mood for gossip. He moved away.

Notary Pecorilla gulped his ice hastily and followed him. They went out to lean over the balcony. The festivities boiled joyously below. Don Luigi vented his bad humor on the festival, and from the festival proceeded to the Mezzogiorno Bank, the Fiat Company, the Government, the Vatican, and the United Nations. "We've been had, all of us," he said, in conclusion.

"Is something going badly for you?" the notary inquired.

"Everything," Don Luigi answered.

"The two of us should have a talk," the notary said.

"What good does it do to talk?" Don Luigi said wearily. "What I know, you know and everyone else knows. Why talk about it?"

"I'm curious. And I've got to get it off my chest. If I can't get something off my chest with you, whom I've known for sixty years, then with whom can I? These things I don't even talk to my wife about."

"Let's go outside," Don Luigi said.

"To my office," the notary suggested.

The notary's office was two steps away, on the ground floor. They went in; the notary lighted the light and closed the door. They sat down facing each other and scrutinized each other without a word. Then Don Luigi said, "You brought me here to talk. Talk."

The notary hesitated, then precipitately, as if he were stripping off a sliver of skin, he said with an effort but firmly, "The poor pharmacist had nothing to do with it."

"What a discovery!" Don Luigi said. "I realized how things stood before the three days of mourning were over."

"You realized or you knew?"

"I knew one thing that made me realize what lay behind the appearances."

"And what did you know?"

"That Roscio had discovered his wife's infidelity with her cousin. He had caught them together."

"Right. That's what I learned, too. Perhaps later than you, but I knew it."

"I knew it right away because the maid at the Roscios' is the mother of my Aunt Clotilda's maid."

"Ah, yes. . . . But what I mean is, when Roscio discovered his wife in—let's say in sweet converse with the other man, what did he do?"

"He didn't do anything. He turned and walked away."

"Christ Almighty! How could he have left them alive and breathing? I'd have slaughtered them."

"Stuff and nonsense. Here, in this homeland of jealousy and honor, you find the most perfect specimens of the betrayed husband. And then, the fact is, the poor doctor was mad about his wife."

"And I can tell you the sequel, because I have it at first hand. The sacristan at the mother church told me, but I must ask you—"

"You know me. I don't talk. Not even if they were to put me on the grid."

"Well, for about a month Roscio said nothing. Then, one day, he went to see the Dean, told him about the infidelity he had discovered, and gave him an ultimatum: either he would send his nephew away, out of town, and see to it that he never came back, or he—Roscio—would hand over to a friend of his, a Communist deputy, certain documents that would send his wife's lover packing off to jail."

"How did he get hold of the documents?"

"It seems he went to Rosello's office one day when he wasn't in. The assistant, the young fellow in the office, showed him in and left him there alone. Roscio knew that the lawyer was out of town and wouldn't be coming back, but he insisted that Rosello had given him an appointment.

It was past noon, and the boy had to go to lunch; further-more, he didn't know the relationship between the lawyer and doctor had changed; he supposed they were very close, as usual. So he left Roscio there alone, and Roscio pro-ceeded to photograph Lord knows what. . . . I say photo-graph because it's certain that Rosello didn't realize, didn't know anything, until Roscio talked with the Dean. So when the Dean told him what Roscio had in his possession, Ro-sello flew to question the boy. The boy remembered the visit and said that, yes, he had left the doctor alone in the office. At that, Rosello's nerves snapped; he slapped the boy and fired him. Then he had second thoughts, went to find him, explained that he had lost his temper because Roscio had complained about having been made to wait uselessly, and that the appointment had been important. He gave the boy ten thousand lire and took him back."

"The sacristan told you all this?"

"No, this part I learned from the boy's father."

"But did Rosello keep such important papers lying about within anyone's reach?"

"This I don't know. Roscio might have had a duplicate key. And then Rosello has been having his own sweet way for so many years, and scot-free at that, so perhaps he thought he was safe, untouchable. . . . But when his uncle told him about Roscio's either/or, he felt the ground slip-ping from under his feet."

"Exactly," Don Luigi agreed. "My Aunt Clotilda, on the other hand, maintains that Roscio was got rid of because the lovers could no longer hide, pretend. . . . Passion, in a word."

"Passion my foot," the notary said. "They were used to the deception. The affair had started when they came home from college for vacation. First they did it secretly at the Dean's house, and later in the husband's house, and maybe they enjoyed it that way—there's the excitement of the forbidden thing, the danger—"

He interrupted himself because someone was knocking at the door: light but persistent little knocks. "Now, who can that be?" the notary asked worriedly.

"Open the door and see," Don Luigi said.

The notary went to open the door. It was Commendatore Zerillo. "What's this?" he said. "You leave the party and come shut yourselves up in here?"

"Mmm," the notary said coldly.

"What were you talking about?"

"The weather."

"Let well enough alone. The weather's good for the moment and there's no need to talk about it. . . . Let me make myself clear. If I don't talk to somebody, I'm going to burst, and you two were talking about exactly the things I've got here." He rubbed his open hand over the top of his stomach, and ground his teeth as if he were in uncontrollable pain.

"If you really can't stand any more, go ahead. We're all ears," Don Luigi said.

"You two won't talk?"

"What should we say?" the notary asked, with an innocent air.

"Let's put the cards on the table. You were talking about this engagement, and about Roscio and the pharmacist—"

"Not in your wildest dreams."

". . . and about that poor Professor Laurana," the Commendatore continued, "who disappeared like Antonio Patò in *Mortorio*."

Fifty years before, during a performance of *Mortorio*—that is, the Passion of Christ, according to Cavalier D'Orioles—Antonio Patò, who was playing Judas, had disappeared, as the part called for him to do, through the trap door that was punctually opened, just as it had been hundreds of times before in rehearsals and performances; only, and this was not in the script, from that moment on no one had ever seen him again. The incident had passed over into folklore to illustrate mysterious disappearances of people or things. The harking back to Patò, therefore, aroused the hilarity of Don Luigi and the notary, but they quickly composed themselves, put on serious, innocent, concerned faces, and, avoiding Zerillo's eye, Don Luigi asked, "What's Laurana got to do with it?"

"Two poor little innocents," the Commendatore soothed them ironically. "Poor innocents who know nothing, say nothing. . . . Look, see this finger? Bite it!" He brought close to the mouth first of the notary and then of Don Luigi his clenched right hand, with only the little finger extended, the way, in the less antiseptic days of our ancestors, mothers used to do with children who were teething.

All three laughed. Then Zerillo said, "I found out something, something that must remain among the three of us. I rely on you. . . . It's got to do with poor Laurana—"

"He was an ass," Don Luigi said.

ABOUT THE AUTHOR

Leonardo Sciascia, Sicily's most discussed writer of the moment, was born in Recalmuto, Italy, in 1921. He received his teaching degree in 1941 from the Diplomato Scuola Magistrale. His teaching career was delayed, however, by the upheavals of war until 1949, when he took a position in a public elementary school in Sicily.

As a native of the locale, Sciascia is able to convey the mysterious Sicilian personality with its repugnance to change and hostility to authority, qualities which often seem archaic to the objective observer. This identification with his homeland has marked everything Mr. Sciascia has written since 1956, when he published *The Parishes of Regalpetra*, a description of his native village. Since that time, besides some stories, sketches, a play, and an essay on Pirandello, he has written several notable short novels. *Mafia Vendetta, The Council of Egypt*, and *A Man's Blessing* have been published in the United States.

Today Mr. Sciascia lives with his wife and two daughters in Palermo, Sicily.

Format by Katharine Sitterly
Set in Linotype Electra
Composed and printed by York Composition Co., Inc.
Bound by The Haddon Craftsmen, Inc.
HARPER & ROW, PUBLISHERS, INCORPORATED